P9-DNP-590

Ways of Dying

WITHDRAWN

Ways of Dying *a novel*

ZAKES MDA

Picador USA

Farrar, Straus and Giroux
New York

WAYS OF DYING. Copyright © 1995 by Zakes Mda. Copyright © Oxford University Press Southern Africa 1991. All rights reserved. Printed in the United States of America. No part of this book may be used or reproduced in any manner whatsoever without written permission except in the case of brief quotations embodied in critical articles or reviews. For information, address Picador USA, 175 Fifth Avenue, New York, N.Y. 10010.

www.picadorusa.com

Picador® is a U.S. registered trademark and is used by Farrar, Straus and Giroux under license from Pan Books Limited.

For information on Picador USA Reading Group Guides, as well as ordering, please contact the Trade Marketing department at St. Martin's Press.
Phone: 1-800-221-7945 extension 763
Fax: 212-677-7456
E-mail: trademarketing@stmartins.com

Library of Congress Cataloging-in-Publication Data

Mda, Zakes.
    Ways of dying : a novel / Zakes Mda. 1st Picador USA ed.
        p. cm.
    ISBN 0-312-42091-9
    1. Funeral rites and ceremonies—Fiction. 2. Weepers (Mourners)—Fiction. 3. South Africa—Fiction. 4. Blacks—Fiction. 5. Grief—Fiction. 6. Death—Fiction. I. Title.

PR9369.3.M4 W39 2002
823'914—dc21   2002066772

First published in South Africa by Oxford University Press Southern Africa

First Picador USA Edition: August 2002

10 9 8 7 6 5 4 3 2 1

Ways of Dying

I

'There are many ways of dying!' the Nurse shouts at us. Pain is etched in his voice, and rage has mapped his face. We listen in silence. 'This our brother's way is a way that has left us without words in our mouths. This little brother was our own child, and his death is more painful because it is of our own creation. It is not the first time that we bury little children. We bury them every day. But they are killed by the enemy ... those we are fighting against. This our little brother was killed by those who are fighting to free us!'

We mumble. It is not for the Nurse to make such statements. His duty is to tell how this child saw his death, not to give ammunition to the enemy. Is he perhaps trying to push his own political agenda? But others feel that there is no way the Nurse can explain to the funeral crowd how we killed the little brother without parading our shame to the world. That the enemy will seize hold of this, and use it against us, is certainly not the Nurse's fault. Like all good Nurses, he is going to be faithful to the facts.

Toloki belongs to the section of the crowd that believes strongly in the freedom of the Nurse to say it as he sees it. He has been to many funerals, and has developed admiration for those who are designated the Nurse at these rituals. They are the fortunate ones, those who were the last to see the deceased alive. Usually they are a fountain of fascinating information about ways of dying.

He moves forward a bit, for he wants to hear every word. The muttering about the Nurse's indiscretion has become so loud that it is beginning to swallow his words of anger. Toloki thought he would need to elbow his way through the crowd, but people willingly move away from him. Why do people give way? he wonders. Is it perhaps out of respect for his black costume and top hat, which he wears at every funeral as a hallmark of his profession? But then why do they cover their noses and mouths with their hands as they retreat in blind panic, pushing those behind them? Maybe it is the beans he ate for breakfast. They say it helps if you put some sugar in them, and he had no sugar. Or maybe it is the fact that he has not bathed for a whole week, and the December sun has not been gentle. He has been too busy attending funerals to go to the beach to use the open showers that the swimmers use to rinse salt water from their bodies.

'Merrie kressie, ou toppie,' whispers a drunk, the only one who is not intimidated by whatever it is that people seem to fear from his presence. Merry Christmas, old man. Old man? He is only thirty-eight years old. He might even be younger than the drunk. 'It is the perfume, ou toppie. It is too strong.' He hears a woman snigger. Why would anyone hate his sacred fragrance? It is the perfume that he splashes all over his body as part of the ritual of his profession before he goes to a funeral. On this fiery Christmas day, its strong smell is exacerbated by the stench of sweat, not only from his body, but from those in the crowd as well.

Toloki is now very close to the makeshift podium where the Nurse defiantly stands, but he still cannot hear a word he is trying to say. Some of us are heckling the Nurse. Some are heckling the hecklers. So, we do not hear one another. Toloki never thought he would live to see the day when a Nurse would be heckled. This is a sacrilege that has never been heard of before. And at the funeral of an innocent little boy, on a Christmas Day too.

Then he sees her, the mother of the boy. She is a convulsion of sobs, and is surrounded by women who try to comfort her.

She lifts her eyes appealingly to the feuding crowd, and Toloki thinks he has seen those eyes before. But how can it be? He must approach and speak with her. Only then can he be sure. But people close around her and stop him.

'I just want to speak with her.'

'We know who you are. You are Toloki the Professional Mourner. We do not need your services here. We have enough of our own mourners.'

'It is not on a professional basis that I want to see her. Please let me speak with her.'

'Ha! You think you are going to convince her behind our backs to engage your services? I can tell you we have no fees to pay a Professional Mourner. We can mourn just as well.'

Who are these people, anyway, who won't let him see the woman he strongly suspects is from his home village? He learns that they are members of her street committee. They are determined to protect her from all those who want to harass her with questions about the death of her son. Newspaper reporters have been particularly keen to get close to her, to ask her silly questions such as what her views are on the sorry fact that her son was killed by his own people. They are keen to trap her into saying something damaging, so that they can have blazing headlines the next day. The street committee is always vigilant.

The Nurse cannot go on to tell us the story of the death of the deceased, this our little brother. The din is too loud. The church minister says a quick prayer. Spades and shovels eat into the mound of earth next to the grave, and soon the hole that will be the resting place of this our little brother forever more amen is filled up. Those nearest the grave sing a hymn, while a man with a shovel delicately shapes the smaller mound that has risen where the hole used to be. Wreaths are laid. Someone wants to know if the messages on the wreaths will not be read for the public as is customary, and in any case where are the relatives of this bereaved mother? She has no relatives, someone else shouts back. The street committee are her relatives. Then a procession led by the van that had brought the coffin to the graveyard is formed, in preparation for the solemn march back to the home of the mother of the deceased in the squatter camp, where we will wash our hands and feast on the food that has been prepared by the street committee.

Toloki decides that he will rush to the home of the deceased, wash his hands and disappear from the scene. He will have nothing to do with people who have treated him with so much disrespect. Hungry as he is, he will not partake of their food either. If he did not have so much reverence for funeral rituals, he would go home right away, without even washing his hands. People give way as he works his way to the head of the procession, which is already outside the gates of the cemetery. By the time he gets to the street, the procession has come to a standstill, and people are impatiently complaining about the heat. Others attempt to sing hymns, but their voices have gone hoarse from the graveyard feud. Those who can still come up with a feeble note or two are overwhelmed by blaring hooters in the street.

These come from a wedding procession of many cars and buses, all embellished with colourful ribbons and balloons. They are going in the opposite direction, and will not give way to the funeral procession. The funeral procession will not give way either, since out of respect for the dead, it is customary for funeral processions to have the right of way. The wedding party is enjoying the stalemate, and they sing at the top of their voices. Their heads, and sometimes half their colourfully clad bodies, appear from the windows of the cars and buses, and they beat the sides of these vehicles with their hands, creating a tumultuous rhythm. The driver of the convertible car in front, which carries the bride and the bridegroom, argues with the driver of the van which carries the mother of the dead child.

'You must give way!'

'But we are a funeral procession.'

'We are a procession of beautiful people, and many posh cars and buses, while yours is an old skorokoro of a van, and hundreds of ragged souls on foot.'

'It is not my fault that these people are poor.'

No one will budge. There might be a violent confrontation here, since the driver of the convertible, who is a huge fellow, is beginning to call certain parts of the van driver's mother that the slight van driver never even knew she had. Toloki walks to the convertible. He greets the bridal couple, and is about to give them a stern lecture on funeral etiquette, when the ill-humoured driver of the convertible suddenly decides that he will give way after all. He signals to the other drivers in the wedding procession to park on the side of the road so that the funeral procession can pass peacefully. Toloki smiles. He has this effect on people sometimes. Perhaps it is his fragrance. And the black costume and top hat of his profession. It cannot be that the driver of the convertible is intimidated by his size. He is quite short, in fact. But what he lacks in height he makes up for in breadth. He is quite stockily built, and his shoulders are wide enough to comfortably bear all the woes of bereavement. His yellow face is broad and almost flat, his pointed nose hovers over and dwarfs his small child-like mouth. His eyes are small, and have a permanently sorrowful look that is most effective when he musters up his famous graveside manner. Above his eyes rest thick eyebrows, like the hairy thithiboya caterpillar.

The driver of the van approaches him. 'The mother of the child we have just buried wants to thank you for what you have done.'

So he goes to the van, and his suspicion is confirmed. He has no doubt that this is Noria, the beautiful stuck-up bitch from his village. She has grown old now, and has become a little haggard. But she is still beautiful. And she too recognises him.

'Toloki! You are Toloki from the village!'

'Yes, Noria, it is me. I wanted to see you at the graveyard, but they wouldn't let me get near you.'

'You can't blame them, Toloki. Ever since my son died, all sorts of people have been pestering us.'

Then she invites him to come and see her at the squatter camp when the sad business of the funeral is over. Toloki walks away with a happy bounce in his feet. He will wash his hands and leave quickly. He will see Noria tomorrow, or maybe the day after. My God! Noria! He has not seen her for almost twenty years! How old would she be now? She must be thirty-five. He remembers that he was three years older. A hard life has taken its toll since she left the village. But her beauty still remains.

* * *

It is not different, really, here in the city. Just like back in the village, we live our lives together as one. We know everything about everybody. We even know things that happen when we are not there; things that happen behind people's closed doors deep in the middle of the night. We are the all-seeing eye of the village gossip. When in our orature the storyteller begins the story, 'They say it once happened ...', we are the 'they'. No individual owns any story. The community is the owner of the story, and it can tell it the way it deems it fit. We would not be needing to justify the communal voice that tells this story if you had not wondered how we became so omniscient in the affairs of Toloki and Noria.

Both Toloki and Noria left the village at different times, and were bent on losing themselves in the city. They had no desire to find one another, and as a result forgot about the existence of each other. But we never stopped following their disparate and meagre lives. We were happy when they were happy. And felt the pain when they were hurt. In the beginning, there were times when we tried to get them together, like homeboys and homegirls sometimes get together and talk about home, and celebrate events of common interest such as births, marriages, ancestral feasts, and deaths. But our efforts disappeared like sweat in the hair of a dog. Indeed, even in his capacity as a Professional Mourner, Toloki avoided funerals that involved homeboys and homegirls. Since his bad experience with Nefolovhodwe, the furniture-maker who made it good in the city, and now pretends that he does not know the people from the village anymore, Toloki has never wanted to have anything to do with any of the people of his village who have settled in the city. He is not the type who forgives and forgets, even though his trouble with Nefolovhodwe happened many years ago, during his very early days in the city. Noria, on the other hand, has always lived in communion with her fellow-villagers, and with other people from all parts of the country who have settled in the squatter camp. So, we put the idea of getting Noria and Toloki together out of our minds until today, at the funeral of this our little brother.

* * *

The distant bells of the cathedral toll 'Silent Night', as Toloki prepares to sleep for the night. The strikes are slow and painful, not like the cheery carol that the angel-faced choirboys sang that very morning on the steps of the church. He was on his way to the funeral, and he stopped and listened. Christmas Day has no real significance for him. Nor has the church. But he enjoys carols, and always sings along whenever he hears them. He could not stop for long, since he did not know what time the funeral would be. He was not involved in this funeral in his professional capacity. In fact, until that morning he was not aware that there was going to be a funeral on this day. It is not usual to hold funerals on Christmas Day. He thought he was doomed to sit in utter boredom at his quayside resting place for the entire day, sewing his costume and putting his things in readiness for the busy coming days in the cemeteries. Then he heard two dockworkers talk of the strange things that were happening these days, of this woman whose child was killed, and who insisted that he must be buried on Christmas Day or not at all. Toloki there and then decided to seize the opportunity, and spend a fulfilling day at the graveside. He did not have an inkling that a homegirl was involved in this funeral, otherwise we know that he would not have gone. But after all, he was happy to see Noria.

At regular intervals of one hour the bell tolls 'Silent Night'. At the window of the tower, perhaps in the belfry, Toloki can see a Christmas tree with twinkling lights of red, green, blue, yellow, and white. The cathedral is a few streets away from his headquarters, as he calls the quayside shelter and waiting-room where he spends his nights. But since it is on a hill, he can enjoy the beauty of the lights, and tonight the bells will lull him to a blissful sleep with carols. But first he must prepare some food for himself. From the shopping trolley where he keeps all his worldly possessions, he takes out a packet containing his favourite food, a delicacy of Swiss cake relished with green onions. He pushes the trolley into one corner, where he knows it is always safe. Though his headquarters are a public place, no one ever touches his things, even when he has gone to funerals and left them unattended for the whole day. Everyone knows that the trolley belongs to Toloki who sleeps at the quayside, come rain or shine. No one ever bothers him and his property. Not the cleaners, nor the police. Not even the rowdy sailors from cargo ships and the prostitutes who come to entertain them.

14

He takes a bite first of the cake, and then of the green onions. His eyes roll in a dance of pleasure. He chews slowly, taking his time to savour each mouthful. Quite a tingling taste, this delicacy has. It is as though the food is singing in his mouth. Quite unlike the beans that he ate this morning. Those who have seen him eat this food have commented that it is an unusual combination. All the more reason to like it. Although it is of his own composition, it gives him an aura of austerity that he associates with monks of eastern religions that he has heard sailors talk about.

Sometimes he transports himself through the pages of a pamphlet that he got from a pink-robed devotee who disembarked from a boat from the east two summers ago, and walks the same ground that these holy men walk. He has a singularly searing fascination with the lives of these oriental monks. It is the thirst of a man for a concoction that he has never tasted, that he has only heard wise men describe. He sees himself in the dazzling light of the aghori sadhu, held in the same awesome veneration that the devout Hindus show the votaries. He spends his sparse existence on the cremation ground, cooks his food on the fires of a funeral pyre, and feeds on human waste and human corpses. He drinks his own urine to quench his thirst. The only detail missing is a mendicant's bowl made from a human skull, for he shuns the collection of alms. Votary or no votary, he will not collect alms. It is one tradition of the sacred order that he will break, in spite of the recognition of the shamanistic elements of almstaking. When he comes back to a life that is far from the glamour of the aghori sadhu in those distant lands, he is glad that even in his dreams he is strong enough not to take a cent he has not worked for. In his profession, people are paid for an essential service that they render the community. His service is to mourn for the dead.

He curls up on the bench and sleeps in the foetal position that is customary of his village. Although he has been in the city for all these years, he has not changed his sleeping position, unlike people like Nefolovhodwe who have taken so much to the ways of the city that they sleep in all sorts of city positions. In all fairness, he has not seen Nefolovhodwe in his sleep, but a man like him who pretends not to know people from his village anymore now that he is one of the wealthiest men in the land, is bound to sleep with his legs straight or in some such absurd position. Unlike the village people, Toloki does not sleep naked however, because his headquarters are a public place. He sleeps fully-dressed, either in his professional costume or in the only other set of clothes that he owns, which he calls home clothes. Since his mourning costume is getting old, and the chances of his getting another one like it are very slim indeed, he often changes into his home clothes in the public toilet as soon as he arrives back from the funerals. He would like to save his costume, so that it lasts for many more years of mourning. This is December, and the weather is very hot and clammy. So he does not cover himself with a blanket. For the winters, when the icy winds blow from the ocean, he is armed with a thick blanket that he keeps in his shopping trolley.

Sleep does not come easily, even with the hourly lullaby of the bells. He thinks of the events of today. Of course he is piqued. What self-respecting Professional Mourner wouldn't be? Why did they treat him so at this boy's funeral? He is well-known and well-liked all over the city cemeteries. Only yesterday he surpassed himself at the funeral of a man who died a mysterious death.

Normally when he is invited to mourn by the owners of a corpse, he sits very conspicuously on the mound that will ultimately fill the grave after prayers have been made and the Nurse has spoken, and weeps softly for the dead. Well, sometimes the Nurse and other funeral orators speak at the home of the corpse, or in church if the corpse was a Christian in its lifetime, before it is taken to the graveyard. But in any case, he sits on the mound and shares his sorrow with the world. The appreciative family of the deceased pays him any amount it can. One day he would like to have a fixed rate of fees for different levels of mourning, as in other professions. Doctors have different fees for different illnesses. Lawyers charge fees which vary according to the gravity of the case. And certainly these professionals don't accept just any amount the client feels like giving them. But for the time being he will accept anything he is given, because the people are not yet used to the concept of a Professional Mourner. It is a fairly new concept, and he is still the only practitioner. He would be willing to train other people though, so that when he dies the tradition will continue. Then he will live in the books of history as the founder of a noble profession.

Yesterday saw the highlight of a career that has spanned quite a few years. As we have told you, the man in question died a mysterious death. The family of the deceased gave Toloki a huge retainer to grace the funeral with his presence. It was the biggest amount he had ever received for any one funeral. Not even at mass funerals had he earned such an amount. So, he made a point of giving of his very best. Throughout the funeral, orator after orator, he sat on the mound and made moaning sounds of agony that were so harrowing that they affected all those who were within earshot, filling their eyes with tears. When the Nurse spoke, he excelled himself by punctuating each painful segment of her speech with an excruciating groan that sent the relatives into à frenzy of wailing.

The Nurse explained that no one really knew how this brother died. What qualified her to be the Nurse was not that she was the last person to see him alive; she was the only person who went out of her way to seek the truth about his death, and to hunt his corpse down when everyone else had given up.

People should therefore not expect of her what they normally expected of the Nurse: to hear the exact details of what ailed this brother, of how he had a premonition of his death, of how he died, and of what last words he uttered before his spirit left the body.

This our elder brother, we learnt from the Nurse, left home one day and said he was visiting his beloved sister, who now found herself standing before this grieving multitude in the person of the Nurse. But since the day he stepped out of the door of his house, no one had seen him alive again. For the first two days, his wife and four children did not worry unduly. 'After all,' said the Nurse, 'men are dogs, and are known to wander from time to time.'

Now, this part was not pleasant to the ears of the men. 'How can a young girl who still smells her mother's milk say such disrespectful slander about us? What kind of an upbringing is this?' they grumbled among themselves. But the Nurse brazenly continued on the scandalous behaviour of the male species. Then she went on to say that after two days, the wife phoned the sister, and all the other relatives, but none of them had seen him. He had never reached his sister's house. As is the practice, they searched all the hospitals in the area, and all the police stations and prisons. None of them had any information about their brother. This was a process that took many days, since prisons and hospitals were teeming with people whose relatives didn't even know that they were there, and the bureaucrats who worked at these places were like children of one person. They were all so rude, and were not keen to be of assistance to people – especially to those who looked poor. 'And you know what?' the Nurse fumed, 'these are our own people. When they get these big jobs in government offices they think they are better than us. They treat us like dirt!'

The family sat down together and decided that this brother was lost, and there was nothing that could be done. But his sister said, 'How can a human being be lost when he is not a needle? I say someone somewhere knows where my brother is. We have not even completed the custom of searching. We have not gone to the mortuary.'

And so she went to the big government mortuary. There were many people there, also looking for relatives who were missing and might be dead. She joined the queue in the morning when the offices opened. At last her turn came at midday. The woman at the counter looked at her briefly, and then took a pen and doodled on a piece of paper. Then she shouted to a girl at the other end of the office, and boasted to her about the Christmas picnic she and her friends were going to hold. They discussed dresses, and the new patterns that were in vogue. They talked of the best dressmakers, who could sew dresses that were even more beautiful than those found in the most exclusive and expensive city boutiques specializing in Italian and Parisian fashions. The girl said she was going out to the corner cafe to buy fat cakes, and the woman at the counter said, 'Bring me some as well.' Then she went back to her doodling. A kindly old man standing behind this our sister who was looking for her beloved brother whispered, 'My daughter, maybe you should remind her royal highness that we are all waiting for her assistance.'

'Miss, I am looking for my brother.'

'Oh, is that so? I thought you were paying us a social visit, because I see you just standing there staring at me.'

She was led by a white-coated official to a corridor where there were a dozen corpses lying naked on the floor. None of these were her brother. She was led to another room, with more naked bodies on the floor. These, she was told, had just been delivered that morning. Altogether there were perhaps twenty bodies of old and young men and women, beautiful girls with stab wounds lying in grotesque positions, children who were barely in their teens, all victims of the raging war

19

consuming our lives. 'I tell you, mothers and fathers, there is death out there. Soon we shall experience the death of birth itself if we go on at this rate.' People were not thrilled at the Nurse's constant editorializing. They wanted her to get to the marrow of the story: how she got the corpse of this our brother. But she felt that these things had to be said nevertheless.

The white-coated official led her to another room with corpses in trays almost like oversized filing cabinets. It was a very cold room. The official said, 'Most of these are the bodies of unidentified persons. I can only open two trays at a time, and then we must run away quickly to get to the warmth of the sun outside. If we don't, we'll freeze to death in here.' And so he opened two trays, and she looked at the bodies. She shook her head, and they rushed out to stand in the sun. After a few minutes, they went inside again and repeated the process. It was obvious that this procedure was going to take many days. The fact that new corpses were brought in all the time, while others were taken out for burial, complicated things. But she was prepared to go through all the distress, even though her stomach was turning, and she was salivating, ready to throw up. It was late in the afternoon, and she had gone through the procedure more than ten times when a saviour came in the form of another white-coated official who looked senior both in years and in rank. 'You can identify your brother by the clothes he was wearing,' he said. He explained that all the clothes that the dead people were wearing were stacked in a room, with numbers on them corresponding to the numbers on the trays.

The sister did not know what clothes her brother was wearing. After phoning his wife, who described them to her, she went to the pile of clothes. She was relieved to find them there after just a few minutes of looking; relieved not because her brother was dead, but because at last the search was over. 'These are the clothes my brother was wearing when he was last seen by his family,' she told the official. They went back to the cold room, and the official pulled out the tray. But the body was not there. The tray was empty!

The white-coated official was concerned. On investigating the matter, he found that the body that had been in that tray had been released that morning, obviously by mistake, to a family which lived in another town. It had been given to their undertaker. It was late in the evening, and the only thing the sister could do was to go home and sleep.

The next morning, accompanied by a few male relatives, she got onto a train that took them to the town where her brother's body had been dispatched. To their horror, the body was already in the graveyard, and a funeral service was in progress. A strange-looking man, the very man who could be seen sitting on the mound mourning with them today for their beloved brother, was sitting on a mound in that distant town, weeping softly. The body of their brother was about to be buried by strangers, when they got there and stopped the funeral service.

'What is wrong with these people? What is their trouble?'

'I tell you, people of God, it is a wrong body you are burying there. It is the body of my brother.'

'Who are these people who want to steal our corpse?'

A fight nearly ensued, with the undertaker insisting that it was the right body, and that the madwoman accompanied by her mad delegation must be arrested for disrupting a solemn occasion. But the sister stood her ground. 'Kill me if you will,' she said. 'I am not going away from here until you release the body of my brother.' She was determined that if they refused, they should bury her there with him. The strange-looking man saved the day. 'Please,' he appealed to the indignant crowd, 'let us not desecrate this place where the dead have their eternal sleep by fighting here. It is easy to solve this problem. Open the coffin to prove once and for all that this is the right body.' The undertaker, supported by some members of the family that supposedly owned the corpse, refused and told the minister to continue with the funeral service. But some members of the crowd advised that the coffin be opened so as to avoid the scandal of a fight in the graveyard. The coffin was opened, and indeed this our brother was in it.

Before the delegation took the body home, the sister spoke with the strange-looking man who had helped them by suggesting that the coffin be opened.

'Who are you, father, who have been so helpful?'

'I am Toloki the Professional Mourner.' Then he explained about his profession, and told them that, in fact, this was his very first job in this small town so far away from the city cemeteries where he regularly worked.

'You are a good man. We shall engage your services for the funeral of this our brother.'

'It will be my pleasure to mourn for him a second time.'

That was why they were seeing him there, mourning his heart out.

But this was not all that the Nurse wanted to say about this our brother. The sister had gone further in investigating who had brought her brother's body to the mortuary. It was brought in by the police, she found. She went to the police station to inquire where the police had found her brother's body. It was found, she was told, near a garage next to the hostels where migrant workers from distant villages lived. In the morning, the garage nightwatchman noticed something that was not there the previous night. He went closer and discovered a man's body. The head had been hacked open, and the brain was hanging out. There were bullet wounds on the legs. He phoned the police, who came and took the body. They said more bodies with similar wounds had been found nearby. They were all packed into the police van and dumped in the mortuary.

'Yes, it must be the migrant workers from the hostels,' various people in the crowd shouted angrily. 'They have killed a lot of our people, and all we do is sit here and keep on talking peace. Are we men or just scared rats?'

There was no one who did not know that the vicious migrants owed their allegiance to a tribal chief who ruled a distant village with an iron fist. They came to the city to work for their children, but the tribal chief armed them, and sent them out to harass the local residents. Sometimes they were even helped by the police, because it helped to suppress those who were fighting for freedom. Nobody seemed to know exactly why the tribal chief did these ugly things, or where his humanity had gone. But others in the crowd said that it was because he wanted to have power over all the land, instead of just his village. He wanted to rule everybody, not just his villagers, even though he did not have support from the people. Throughout the land people hated him and wished him dead. People knew who their real leaders were, the crowd said, and if the tribal chief wanted to play a rough game, then he would find himself facing his age-mates.

This politicking was interfering with Toloki's inspired mourning. He calmed the crowd down, and told them to concentrate on the business of mourning. Although the issues that the people were angry about were important, they could always discuss them when they got back to the squatter camps and townships. They had grassroots leadership in the form of street committees, which had always been effective in calling meetings to discuss matters of survival and self-defence. Everybody in the crowd agreed with him. He felt very proud of the fact that people had listened to his advice. Perhaps he was gaining more importance in the eyes of the community. Before these incidents where he found himself actually acting in an advisory capacity, his role had been to mourn, and only to mourn. He must keep his priorities straight, however. The work of the Professional Mourner was to mourn, and not to intervene in any of the proceedings of the funeral. It would lower the dignity of the profession to be involved in human quarrels.

* * *

That was yesterday. Today he was treated with the utmost disrespect, and now he is annoyed. He sleeps, and in his dreams he sees the sad eyes of Noria, looking appealingly at the bickering crowd.

2

Toloki opens his eyes. Boxing Day. One of those senseless holidays when we do not bury our dead. Like Christmas Day. Instead we go for what we call a joll. All it means is that we engage in an orgy of drinking, raping, and stabbing one another with knives and shooting one another with guns. And we call it a joll. We walk around the streets, pissing in our pants, and shouting, 'Happee-ee-e!' That's what Christmas is all about. And Boxing Day is the day we go out to bars and shebeens to take off the hangover of yesterday. But by midday, the whole orgy has started all over again. Some of us, the better-off ones, go out to the beach to play volleyball and frisbees, and to piss and vomit on the golden sands as the day gets older. It was just sheer luck that there was a funeral yesterday: only because that stuck-up bitch Noria was sensible enough to insist that her son be buried on Christmas Day, and not on any other day. The street committee, or whoever is in charge of the lives of the squatter-camp dwellers, could have refused, but they acceded to her wish. It just shows how much power Noria still has — especially over men.

Today he must go and see her. Fortunately he is still wearing his professional costume, since he was too lazy to change into his home clothes when he came back from the funeral yesterday. He really must discipline himself to change, and not to sleep in his costume. Otherwise it will get finished, and God knows where he will get another one like it. It was not easy getting this one. One day, years ago, he was passing by one of the city shopping malls. At the paved square where there were flowers and small trimmed trees growing in giant concrete pots, and genteel people sitting at the small round tables eating all sorts of food, he saw a small shop that he had not noticed before. It was between the two restaurants where the pavement diners had ordered their food. Different types of costumes were displayed at the window, and he was struck by a particularly beautiful outfit all in black comprising a tall shiny top hat, lustrous tight-fitting pants, almost like the tights that the young women wear today, and a knee-length velvety black cape buckled with a hand-sized gold-coloured brooch with tassels of yellow, red and green. He fell in love with it. He knew immediately that it would be most suitable for his new vocation which he had decided on only the previous day after his disagreement with Nefolovhodwe.

Toloki walked inside the shop, and was welcomed with a firm handshake by the old man who owned the shop, and his son, who was being trained in the trade. The old man explained to him that his shop served the theatre world. Most of his outfits were period costumes that actors and producers came to rent for plays that were about worlds that did not exist anymore. But other costumes did not belong to any world that ever existed. These were strange and fantastic costumes that people rented for fancy dress balls, or for New Year carnivals, or to make people laugh. Toloki asked him about his favourite outfit in the window. 'Oh, that one,' said the old man. 'I have only rented it out once before, to some Americans who wanted it for a Halloween party.'

'Can I buy it?'

'Buy it? Of course. Although God knows what you'll be buying it for. People don't normally buy these costumes. They rent them because they are things you use only once, and never again.'

'I want to own it.'

But when he heard what the price was, he knew he could not afford it in a hundred years. It was expensive, he was told, because it was made of very expensive material: silk and velvet. He left with a very painful heart, for he really wanted that costume. He could see himself in it, an imposing (albeit stocky) figure in some of the greatest cemeteries of the world, practising his vocation which was slowly taking shape in his mind.

He went back to the shop every day, and sat outside that window looking longingly at the costume. Leaking from his open mouth were izincwe, the gob of desire. The owners of the two restaurants began to complain. 'He is frightening our customers away,' they said. 'Who would want to eat our food while looking at the slimy saliva hanging out of his mouth?' But Toloki refused to move away. It was a public place, wasn't it? Didn't he have a right to be where he wanted to be? At least if he couldn't afford to buy the costume, he had all the right in the world to sit there for the rest of his life and admire it. 'What can we do?' the restaurant owners said resignedly. 'Ever since these people began to know something about rights they have got out of hand. I tell you, politics has destroyed this country.' So, day after day Toloki came to admire his costume, until one day the restaurant owners decided to buy it for him. 'Promise us that if we buy you this costume you will never come back here again,' they begged. He promised, and left happily with the nicely wrapped costume under his arm. He was never seen there again.

That was several years ago. Now the costume has seen better days. The colourful tassels are gone. The topper is crooked and crumpled. The velvet of the cape has developed a thick sheen of dirt, and the tights are held together by wires and safety pins. The black beauty has become almost grey. His pride in this venerable costume increases with age, though, like advocates of law who wear their old and tattered gowns with pride as symbols of their seniority in the bar. He will wear it, certainly, when he goes to see Noria, even though he is not on duty. It is a pity that Noria has never seen him in action. One day he would like to impress her with a flourishing display of his mournful expertise.

Maybe he should first go to the beach and take a shower. He has not washed himself for at least one week. Then he will go to Noria's in the afternoon, when people are done with their household chores and are prepared to welcome visitors. On second thoughts, he will not go to the beach. It is Boxing Day and all the beaches are crowded with holidaymakers from the inland provinces who come especially to litter the lovely coastal city at this time of the year. People like to gawk when he showers. The smaller the crowd the better. Perhaps he will take a walk to the waterfront and entertain himself by watching the antics of the buskers and the ridiculous excitement of the tourists who visit the pubs, stores and theatres there. Or he might just as well sit here, watch ships come and go, and think of Noria.

* * *

Noria. The village. His memories have faded from the deep yellow-ochre of the landscape, with black beetles rolling black dung down the slopes, and colourful birds swooping down to feed on the hapless insects, to a dull canvas of distant and misty grey. Now, however, it is all coming back. Pale herdboys, with mucus hanging from the nostrils, looking after cattle whose ribs you could count, on barren hills with patches of sparse grass and shrubs. Streams that flowed reluctantly in summer and happily died in winter. Homesteads of three or four huts each, decorated outside with geometric patterns of red, yellow, blue and white. Or just white-washed all around. One hovel each for the poorest families. In addition to three huts, his homestead had a four-walled tin-roofed stone building with a big door that never closed properly. This was his father's workshop.

His father, a towering handsome giant in gumboots and aging blue overalls, was a blacksmith, and his bellows and the sounds of beating iron filled the air with monotonous rhythms through the day. Jwara, for that was his father's name, earned his bread by shoeing horses. But on some days – Toloki could not remember whether these were specially appointed days, or whether they were days when business was slack – he created figurines of iron and brass. On those days he got that stuck-up bitch, Noria, to sing while he shaped the red-hot iron and brass into images of strange people and animals that he had seen in his dreams. Noria was ten years old, but considered herself very special, for she sang for the spirits that gave Jwara the power to create the figurines. She had been doing it for quite a few years. Although her voice added to the monotony of the bellows and beating metal, we thought it was quite mellifluous. We came and gathered around the workshop, and solemnly listened to her never-changing song. Even the birds forgot about the beetles, and joined the bees hovering over the workshop, making buzzing and chirping sounds in harmony with Noria's song.

The earliest reference to Noria as a stuck-up bitch was first heard some years back when Toloki's mother was shouting at Jwara, her angry eyes green with jealousy, 'You spend all your time with that stuck-up bitch, Noria, and you do not care for your family!'

Noria was seven at the time, and she and Jwara had spent a whole week in the workshop, without eating any food or drinking any water, while he shaped his figurines and she sang. We came and listened, and went back to our houses to eat and to sleep, and came back again to the workshop, and found them singing and shaping figurines. Even the birds and the bees got tired and went to sleep. When they came back the next day, Noria and Jwara were still at it.

Xesibe, Noria's father, came to the workshop, stood pitifully at the door, and pleaded with Jwara, 'Please, Jwara, release our child. She has to eat and sleep.' But Jwara did not respond. Nor did Noria. It was as though they were possessed by the powerful spirits that made them create the figurines. Noria's mother, the willowy dark beauty known to us only as That Mountain Woman, was very angry with Xesibe: 'How dare you, Father of Noria, interfere with the process of creation! Who are you, Father of Noria, to think that a piece of rag like you can have the right to stop my child from doing what she was born to do?' That Mountain Woman had razor blades in her tongue.

Toloki's mother, on the other hand, was furious. There was no more food in the house, and no one could get Jwara to respond to their pleas that he should give them money to buy maize-meal at the general dealer's store. He just went on hammering and hammering to the rhythm of Noria's monotonous song. It was in these circumstances that Toloki's mother, her stout matronly body shaking with anger, uttered the immortal words that gave Noria her stuck-up bitch title, which lived with her from that day onwards.

We know all these things, but Toloki does not remember them. He only knows that as far as his memory can take him, Noria was always referred to as a stuck-up bitch, and was proud of the title. How this came about, he does not know. Nor can he remember how Noria began to sing for his father. This is how it happened: he was eight and she five. They were playing the silly games that children play outside the workshop. Jwara had just finished shoeing the policemen's horses, and was about to put off the fires, and to close the shop. He was looking forward to taking an early break, and joining his old friends, Xesibe and Nefolovhodwe, for a gourd of sorghum beer. Then Noria sang. Jwara found himself overwhelmed by a great creative urge. He took an idle piece of iron, and put it in the fire. When it was red hot, he began to shape it into a strange figure. He amazed himself, because in all his life he had never known that he had such great talent. But before he could finish the figurine, Noria stopped singing, and all of a sudden he could not continue to shape the figure. The great talent, and the urge to create, had left his body. He could not even remember what he was trying to do with that piece of iron. Then in the course of her game with Toloki, Noria sang her childish song again. The song had no meaning at all. But it had such great power in Jwara that he found himself creating the figurine again. From that day, whenever Jwara wanted to create his figurines, he would invite Noria over to the workshop, she would sing her meaningless song, and he would work for hours on end at the figurines. Sometimes new shapes would visit him in his dreams, and he would want to create them the next day. Jwara and Noria did not usually work every day though, and the time that they worked for the whole week was an exception and a record. It was because Jwara's dreams had been particularly crowded the previous night, and he was unable to stop until he had reproduced all the strange creatures with which he had interacted in his sleep.

We were not surprised, really, that Noria had all this power to change mediocre artisans into artists of genius, and to make the birds and the bees pause in their business of living and pay audience to her. In fact, one thing that Toloki used to be jealous about even as a small boy, was that we all loved the stuck-up bitch, for she had such beautiful laughter. We would crowd around her and listen to her laughter. We would make up all sorts of funny things in order to make her laugh. She loved to laugh at funny faces, and some villagers gained great expertise in making them. A particular young man called Rubber Face Sehole knew how to pull all sorts of funny faces, and whenever he was around we knew that we would all be happily feasting on Noria's laughter. So Noria received all the attention, and Toloki none.

It is rumoured that when Noria was a baby, she already had beautiful laughter. We say it is rumoured because it is one of the few things that we do not know for sure. When That Mountain Woman was pregnant she went to give birth in her village in the mountains, as was the custom with a first child. Since we never had anything to do with the mountain people, we only know about the events there from the stories that people told. They said that nursemaids and babysitters used to tickle Noria for the pleasure of hearing her laughter. This went on until her mother had to stop the whole practice after baby Noria developed sores under her armpits. After that, when she was tickled she did not laugh but cried instead, which seemed to spread a cloud of sadness, not only among those who heard her cry, but throughout the whole mountain village.

We felt that Toloki should not have been overly jealous of Noria. Although we always remarked, sometimes in his presence, that he was an ugly child, he was not completely without talent. He was good with crayons, and could draw such lovely pictures of flowers, mountains and huts. Sometimes he drew horses. But he never drew people. Once he was asked to draw a picture of a person, but his hand refused to move. When he went to school, he would just sit there and draw pictures while the teacher was teaching. Come to think of it, neither Toloki nor Noria paid much attention to school work from the very first day they were registered at the village primary school. But then they were not the only children who did not pay much attention to school work. Toloki drew his pictures not only in class during lessons, but also during break when other children were playing football with a tennis ball on the road near the school.

There was the time when a milling company sponsored a national art competition for primary school pupils. Those pictures that conquered the eyes of the judges won prizes of books. One of Toloki's pictures, the only entry from the village, won a prize. The big man from the milling company drove all the way from town to the village primary school to award the prize of books to Toloki. The principal asked all the pupils to assemble in the big stone building that served as a classroom for Standards Three, Four and Five, and also as a church on Sundays, just as they did for the morning prayers, and the prize was awarded in front of everybody. Words were spoken that day that filled Toloki's heart with pride, and for the first time in his life he felt more important than everyone else, including Noria. After school, filled with excitement, he ran home with his new books, and went straight to his father's workshop.

'Father, I have won a national art competition. I got all these books.'

'Good.' Jwara did not look at Toloki, nor at the books. There were no horses to shoe, no figurines to shape. He was just sitting there, staring at hundreds of figurines lined up on the shelves where they were fated to remain for the rest of everybody's lives. And he did not even look at his son.

'Father, I have a picture of a beautiful horse here. It is a dream horse, not like the horses you shoe. Why don't you shape it into a figurine too?'

'Get out of here, you stupid, ugly boy! Can't you see that I am busy?'

Toloki walked out, with tears streaming down his cheeks. How he hated that stuck-up bitch Noria!

If Jwara ruled his household with a rod of iron, he was like clay in the hands of Noria. He bought her sweets from the general dealer's store, and chocolate. Once, when the three friends, Nefolovhodwe, Xesibe and Jwara, were sitting under the big tree in front of Xesibe's house, playing the morabaraba game with small pebbles called cattle, and drinking beer brewed by That Mountain Woman (who always had a good hand in all matters pertaining to sorghum), Xesibe complained, 'You know, Jwara, I think you spoil that child. You pamper her too much with good things, and she is now so big-headed that she won't even listen to me, her own father.' Poor Xesibe, he was not aware that at that very moment That Mountain Woman was sitting on the stoep, not far from the three friends, sifting wheat flour that she was going to knead for bread. She heard her husband's complaint, and she shouted, 'Hey, you Father of Noria! You should be happy for your daughter. You are a pathetic excuse for a father. Or did you want Jwara to buy sweets and chocolate for a thing like you?' She had razor blades in her tongue, That Mountain Woman. Xesibe was ashamed, and his friends were embarrassed for him. Since that day he never complained again, and Noria continued to receive gifts from Jwara. But so not to offend his dear old friend of many years he told her, 'Don't show these to your father. You can show them to your mother, but never to your father.'

It was not only the razor blades that made people wary of That Mountain Woman. It was also because she was different from us, and her customs were strange, since she was from the faraway mountain villages where most of us had never been. We wondered why Xesibe had to go all the way to the mountains to look for a wife, when our village was famous for its beautiful women. That Mountain Woman had no respect for our ways, and talked with men anyhow she liked. When she had just arrived in the village as a new bride, she was held in great awe and admiration for it was said that, way back in the mountains where she came from, she once walked on the rainbow. Of course no one had proof of that. We only had her word for it. But what we knew for sure was that she was good at identifying different curative herbs, and grinding and mixing them, and in boiling them to make potent medicines for all sorts of ailments. Those days she did not practise professionally as a medicine woman though, but helped members of her new family or their friends when they fell ill.

We told many stories about her, especially when women gathered at the river to wash clothes. She did not seem to be bothered. That Mountain Woman had no shame. The story we told every day, with colourful variations depending on who was telling it, originally happened when she was pregnant with Noria. During the later stages of her pregnancy, she went back to her home village in the mountains. It was the custom that she should give birth to her first child among her own people, and be nursed back to health, and be advised about baby care, by her own mother, and by other female relatives in her village. She went to the government clinic every month to be examined by the nurses, and to get the free powdered milk, cooking oil, and oatmeal that were given to pregnant women. Every time the story was told we exclaimed cynically, 'Oh, they have clinics too in the mountain villages!'

During that period a group of health assistants came to the village, and stayed at the clinic. They were young men who were being trained to educate villagers about primary health care. Sometimes they helped the nurses to bandage the wounds of young men who had participated in stick fights, or in brawls that involved beer and women. During the few weeks that they stayed there, the health assistants accumulated quite a reputation in the villages around the clinic, for they went out drinking every night and did naughty things with the young women whose husbands were migrant workers in the mines.

One day That Mountain Woman noticed that the cooking oil and powdered milk were about to run out. The whole family used this food carelessly because they knew that she got it free from the clinic. Even though it was not her day to attend the clinic, she decided she would go all the same. The nurses would shout at her, and tell her that she was meant to come only when her time was due at the end of the month, but she was going to pretend that she had come because she had felt some pains that morning. An added incentive was that she had heard from some of the pregnant women in her village that there was a new type of food being rationed out at the clinic. These were powdered eggs that the villagers referred to as the eggs of a tortoise. They tasted like real hen eggs when you mixed them with water and fried them in cooking oil.

She rode on her father's horse, since the clinic was located in a valley over the hills, which was quite some distance from her own village. It is said that she was eight months pregnant at the time. At the clinic, she joined the queue of pregnant women who were gossiping about the handsome young health assistants who had invaded the valley with a blaze of town sophistication and class. The young women of the valley were gaga about the health assistants, and the men were so angry that they were heard on occasion threatening to castrate the young upstarts who had the morals of pigs. There was a tinge of envy in the voices of the women in the queue, since nature had deprived them, at least for the time being, of the pleasure of enjoying the attentions of the handsome visitors.

The turn of That Mountain Woman came, and she went into the room where she was to be examined by a nurse. At that moment, there was no nurse in the room. She stripped naked, and lay belly upwards on the bed as was the practice, waiting for the nurse to come and palpate her. Instead, one of the health assistants entered the room. She was surprised and ashamed, and tried to cover her nakedness with her hands. But the young man said, 'Don't be afraid of me. I am a doctor.' Then he began to palpate her, and within minutes, the crotch of his pants was on fire. She felt herself relaxing with him, and they introduced themselves to each other.

'You are a beautiful woman. I think I have fallen in love with you.'

'But I am heavy with child!'

'You won't be like that forever.'

That Mountain Woman felt flattered that even in her most shapeless moments, a whole doctor found her attractive. He told her that even though she was pregnant, there would be no problems if they were to decide to seal their newfound love with a bit of adult merriment. 'And I should know, because I am a doctor,' he added.

'There is no way we can meet. I come from the village over the hills.'

'I have a plan. This evening pretend that you are ill. Ask your people to send for me. Tell them that I am the doctor who examined you today, and I am the only one who understands your illness. Then I'll come.'

The health assistant ran away quickly when he heard the footsteps of the nurse in the corridor. 'Don't tell her I was here,' he said. 'Otherwise she will spoil our thing.'

That evening, That Mountain Woman was attacked by strange pangs in her abdominal area. She moaned and wailed and asked for the doctor who had attended her that day. Old women of the village who knew everything about childbirth and all the complications that sometimes occurred in women, came and offered to help. But she cursed them out of the house, and demanded to see no one but the doctor who examined her that day. A horseman was sent to the clinic over the hills, and found the health assistant waiting for just that message. He said, 'Yes, I am the doctor you are looking for. Go back and tell my patient that I'll get the clinic Land Rover and come immediately.' The horseman rode back with the message, and the health assistant went to ask for a Land Rover from the nurse-clinician in charge of the clinic.

'Why do you want the Land Rover at this late hour?'

'We are supposed to hold a meeting with the village health workers in the village over the hills. I need to go there and make arrangements with the chief.'

'You are indeed a hard worker! You are always thinking of your work even after hours. I am surely going to recommend you for promotion when I write my report to the head-office.'

Unfortunately the Land Rover was being used by another nurse-clinician who had gone with some nurses to visit the outposts. What was he going to do, since he had already promised the desirable woman that he was coming? How would he placate the fire that raged in the crotch of his pants? Wearing a white coat, with a stethoscope stolen from the nurse-clinician's office hanging around his neck, our health assistant went to the police station and asked the officers for their Land Rover. He told them that there was an emergency in the village over the hills. 'Don't worry, doctor, we'll take you there ourselves.' And two conscientious policemen drove him to the village over the hills.

He rushed into the rondavel where That Mountain Woman was lying on a mat on the floor, groaning in pain. Grandmothers were all around her, trying to persuade her to chew the herbs that would drive the pain away. He knelt down beside her, and began to palpate her belly. Then in a grave voice he said, 'I don't want to alarm you, grandmothers, but I think we are looking at something very serious here. I must remain alone with the patient. Please go out, and don't let anyone disturb me.'

Soon a crowd had gathered around the hut. The grandmothers had spread it throughout the village that the woman was dying. The miracle doctor who, by the grace of God, happened to be at the clinic over the hills just at the time when his help was needed, was trying to save her life. Wasn't it fortunate that the clinic which had never had a doctor stationed there before, but had always been staffed by nurses and nurse-clinicians, happened to have a doctor at that very moment? Indeed she was a fortunate woman. The crowd grew larger and larger, and at the same time festal chatter grew louder and louder. Soon the doctor would come out and announce what was ailing the poor woman. But minutes passed, and the doctor did not come out. Those people nearest the door thought they heard some delicate moans and heavy breathing leaking out of the door of the rondavel. The poor woman must be suffering so much!

An hour had passed, and everyone was beginning to get worried. Had something terrible happened to the poor woman? Or perhaps to the doctor? A naughty grandmother whose mind was full of dirty thoughts jokingly said, 'Ha! Wasn't it odd that she smiled when the doctor entered?' Then all those who were in the hut when the doctor arrived suddenly remembered that, yes, she did smile.

These idle babblers planted a seed of suspicion in the mind of the woman's father. Ignoring the advice of those around him, who said that if he angered the doctor his daughter might never be cured, he suddenly kicked the door down. He rushed into the hut, followed by those who were nearest the door. Inside the hut they were greeted by a scene that left them sweating with anger and disgust. Those who were outside the hut were amazed to hear screams. Then the doctor was flung through the door like a piece of rag. His pants flew after him, and fell in the midst of giggling schoolgirls. Men used their sticks on him, and he screamed, 'You don't understand, good people! I was using a new method of curing the pains on her!'

But the villagers did not believe in new-fangled remedies that involved nakedness. They would have killed him had it not been for the policemen, who took the disgraced doctor away to beat him up themselves. They were even angrier than the villagers, for they said the fake doctor had wasted their time. The young men of the village were not satisfied with the arrangement. 'Why should the police have the monopoly on beating up this pig? We need our share too.' But who could argue with the dogs of the government, as policemen were known throughout the villages? The last time the villagers saw the naked figure of the doctor, it was being frogmarched in front of the police Land Rover, in the glare of the headlights, and it was screaming, 'Please forgive me, fathers! It was all a mistake! I will never do it again!'

We told the story over and over again, and we laughed, and we said, 'That Mountain Woman has no shame.' But one could detect a smack of envy in our voices when we said that. Those were adventures that would never be seen in our conservative village. Noria was born a month after this incident with the doctor. Six months later, when That Mountain Woman returned to our village with baby Noria on her back, we already knew everything about the scandal. We thought she would be hiding her head in shame, and would at last be a humble person, but no, she continued to be her old brash self. She even laughed when someone, who happened to be braver than the rest of us, asked her discreetly and in well-chosen words about the scandal. That Mountain Woman had no shame.

When Noria was born it was generally believed by the mountain people that her ears looked like those of the doctor. The story spread to our village as well. Though we had never seen him with our own eyes, we strongly believed until this day, that the doctor contributed Noria's ears. The nurses at the clinic tried, to no avail, to explain that Noria could not have the doctor's ears since That Mountain Woman was already eight months pregnant when she had merriment with him. Noria was already formed, with ears and all. But we refused to believe the nurses, who would obviously say anything to protect their colleague. We insisted that Noria's ears were those of the doctor. We all marvelled, 'Xesibe has no features. How did he manage to make such a beautiful girl?' Indeed Noria's father, a stubby man who wore a dirty brown blanket at all times and in all types of weather, had a permanently wry countenance.

* * *

It can be boring just to sit and watch ships come and go, especially on Boxing Day when there are not many ships moving in and out of the harbour. Some come, but they will only be

40

unloaded tomorrow, after the holiday, unless they carry perishable food. But memories of his past fill Toloki's time, so much so that the boisterous noise of the drunken sailors and their prostitutes does not disturb him at all, for he cannot hear it. His thoughts are of Noria and of the village and of the people of the village. When Noria left the village he never thought he would see her again. And later he also left. But now it would seem that his road, and that of Noria, were meant to cross from time to time in this journey of life. They grew up together as children. Come to think of it, at the very first funeral he ever attended back in the village, he was with Noria.

* * *

The first funeral. He was thirteen and Noria was ten. The first Nurse that he saw in his life was the principal of the village primary school where he was a pupil. A schoolgirl, who had been Noria's friend during her life, had died a painful death of the gun. She was the first person that we knew of in our village to be shot dead, and it happened in the city. She had gone there, with other pupils who were in the school choir, to bury another pupil who came from the city to attend the village school where there were no disruptions, but who had unfortunately caught pneumonia and died.

The school principal hired the old bus that travelled between our village and the town. Toloki was among the boys who were sent to town to speak with the owner of the bus. It was his first trip to town, which was about two hours away from the village by bus. It was enchanting for him to walk on the gravel road, and to admire the three stores, the post office, the bank, the milling company, and the secondary school that comprised the town. It was a world that was a far cry from the huts of the village, and the rusty tin-roofed school that doubled as a church on Sundays.

The owner of the bus was quite happy to hire the bus out to the school, but he said, 'The city is very far away. It takes one whole day and one whole night to get there. My bus is very old, but it will manage the journey. I must take it to the garage first so that they service it properly.' This meant that those people who depended on the bus to go to town would not be able to go until the bus came back from the city. However, a lot of people went to town on horseback.

When Toloki got home he told his parents about the death of his schoolmate, and of how he was sent with boys who were much older than him to town to speak with the owner of the bus. The pupil who died was a member of the school choir, like both Toloki and Noria, and so the school choir was going to sing at the funeral. Would his parents allow him to go?

'No, you can't go.'

'Please, father!'

'You are too young.'

'But Noria is going, and she is three years younger than me.'

'Noria has more brains in her little finger than you have in your whole body.'

'Father of Toloki, that was not a nice thing to say to your son. And it is wrong not to allow him to go when all the other children of the school are going.'

'Who are you, Mother of Toloki, to teach me how to bring up my children?'

'But, Father of Toloki …'

'You know I don't argue with women, Mother of Toloki. If you want to be the man of the house, take these pants and wear them. Can't you see that this child of yours is so stupid that he will get lost in the city?'

At the end of it all, Toloki's mother was crying, Jwara was staring blankly at the figurines in his workshop, and Toloki did not go to the city. Noria went though, and in addition to the provisions of a whole chicken and steamed bread that her mother prepared for her, Jwara bought her a quantity of sweets and chocolate. Toloki's mother fumed, 'You did not allow your own son to go, but you are not ashamed to spend all your money on that stuck-up bitch Noria!'

We got the whole story of what happened in the city from the Nurse. The choir from our village sang at the night vigil. The principal himself was the conductor. Under his baton, the choir had that very year won a trophy in the district school choir competitions. At the funeral of their schoolmate, the voices of those children in the tent where the vigil was held were even more dulcet than they were when they won the competition. Nobody knew of them, as they were from a faraway village no one had heard of. People of the city were asking, 'Who are these children who sing like angels?' After the song, a relative of the deceased made a speech and explained that these beautiful children, with such melodic voices and faded gymdresses with patches all over, came from a village where the mother of the deceased had been born. The poor child had been sent there to acquire better education because the children of the city did not want to learn, but preferred to run around the streets, sniffing glue and smoking dagga. But unfortunately God decided to call the poor child to his mansion, since a beautiful plate is never used for eating, but is only displayed to be admired. 'In any case you will hear all the details of this child's death from the Nurse at the funeral tomorrow,' he added. 'I merely wanted to tell you who these angels are.'

After this brief but much appreciated speech, a local choir took the stage and sang. But people did not seem to be interested in it. They wanted the village choir to come back and sing for them. In the meantime, Noria and her friend went outside the tent to get some fresh air.

'You know, Noria, I fear something terrible is going to happen.'

'Something terrible has already happened. We have come to bury our schoolmate.'

'I feel we are going to be attacked. Some people don't like our choir because it is doing well.'

'How can you talk like that?'

'There is nothing we can do about it, Noria. When one is called no one can prevent it. I am going to die laughing.'

While they were standing there laughing, for Noria took the whole thing as a joke, they heard an announcement from the tent that the village choir was going to take the stage again. They went inside the tent, joined the other choir members, and sang their hearts out. The people of the city were moved to tears. A man stood up and said, 'I work for the radio station. I want to record this choir so that we can play its music in one of our choral music programmes. We shall surely go to the village to record this choir.' It was at that moment that a man with a gun stood up and shouted, 'You shall record them in their graves!' People screamed and threw themselves on the floor. The man opened fire and Noria's friend was hit in the chest. She died laughing.

It was at her funeral that Toloki came face to face for the first time with the ritual of the Nurse. When the Nurse related in detail how this our little sister died, and her premonitions, and the last words she uttered, and her final laugh, he was no longer the principal that Toloki knew. He was completely transformed, and his voice was not the voice he used at school, where he was always angry and did not hesitate to make the cane work on the buttocks of naughty boys and girls. When he explained how the bullet had pierced the heart of the innocent girl, we wailed, 'People of the city killed our daughter only because she had a beautiful voice.' He modulated his voice, and it blended well with our wails. For Toloki, who at that time did not have an inkling that his future calling would be in the cemeteries of the very city where they killed this our daughter, it was a magic moment. It was only marred by his parents. When the Nurse spoke about the cruel people of the city who had murdered our child, Jwara whispered aloud to his wife, 'You see why I refused when Toloki wanted to go there, Mother of Toloki?'

'But that stuck-up bitch Noria went there, and you bought her things.'

'Noria is not stupid and ugly like Toloki. She is a child of the gods.'

'If Toloki is stupid and ugly, it is because he has taken after you.'

They were shouting at each other. We stopped them, and told them what a disgrace they were. How could they bring the quarrels of their household to the funeral of an innocent child who had died such a painful death? During all this storm, the Nurse never lost his cool for a moment. Noria stood next to Toloki in stunned silence. Later we said it was good that she did not cry, both for her dead friend, and for her name that was being bandied about at a public funeral, for that would have cast an even heavier blanket of gloom over the village. Toloki was so embarrassed that he wished the ground could open and swallow him, especially when suppressed guffaws were heard from the direction of his schoolmates.

* * *

In the afternoon Toloki walks to the taxi rank, which is on the other side of the downtown area, or what is called the central business district. The streets are empty, as all the stores are closed. He struts like a king, for today the whole city belongs to him. He owns the wide tarmac roads, the skyscrapers, the traffic lights, and the flowers on the sidewalks. That is what he loves most about this city. It is a garden city, with flowers and well-tended shrubs and bushes growing at every conceivable

45

place. In all seasons, blossoms fill the air. Sometimes when he goes to a funeral he picks a flower or two, as long as no one sees him, as you are not supposed to pick the flowers in the city parks, gardens and sidewalks. And that gives him a great idea: he might as well pick a few flowers for Noria. Just to make doubly sure, he looks around, then picks a few zinnias. He would have preferred roses, but he would have had to cross two streets in the opposite direction to get roses. So, zinnias will do. At least they are long-stemmed, and come in different colours.

Like the streets, the taxi rank is empty. Usually there are rows and rows of mini-bus taxis, and dirty urchins touting passengers for this or that taxi. And traders selling cheap jewellery and stolen watches. Or fruit and vegetables. This is where he buys his green onions when he comes back from funerals. Or sometimes, when he has had a good payday, a small packet of dried tarragon, which he likes to chew. And then he crosses the street to his favourite bakery to buy Swiss rolls.

An old kombi arrives and drops off a group of domestic workers and people wearing the blue and white uniforms of the Zion Church. That is the taxi to Noria's squatter camp. He gets into the kombi and takes a back seat. The taxi will not go until it is full. People trickle in, but for some strange reason avoid the back seat. It takes up to thirty minutes to fill all the other seats, and those who come after that have no choice but to take the back seat. They sit facing the other way, trying very hard to give their backs to Toloki, and covering their mouths and noses with handkerchiefs or with their hands.

As the taxi drives out of the city through the winding highway on the hill, his heart pounds even faster with the anticipation of talking with Noria. He wonders what could have killed her son. A bullet from the police maybe? He has been to funerals of children who died from police bullets. Not long ago he mourned at a funeral of a five-year-old girl. The Nurse explained that a police bullet ricocheted off the wall and hit the child who was playing with her mudpies in the yard of her home. We have seen many such cases. Police bullets have a strange way of ricocheting off the walls of township houses, and when they do, there is bound to be a child about whom they never miss.

No, it can't be police bullets. Remember that the graveyard quarrel started when the Nurse blamed our own people for killing the boy. Perhaps it was a death that was similar to that of a six-year-old boy he mourned last week. The Nurse told a gruesome story of how the mother and father were sitting in their living-room watching the news on television, when a picture of an unknown corpse flashed on the screen. It was their son who had been missing for the past two days. He had gone to school in the morning and never came back. The parents had asked his schoolmates about him, but they did not know where he was. Then they went to the police but were told, 'Children go missing every day. There is nothing we can do about it.'

'You mean you won't even try to look?'

'Look where? These children run away from their homes to join terrorists.'

'But he is only six.'

'It is the six-year-olds who throw stones and petrol bombs at us, woman. All we can say is that you people must learn to have more control over your children.'

The body of the little boy was discovered in the veld. He had been castrated, and the killer had also cut open his stomach, and had mutilated the flesh from his navel right down to his thighs. The police who were called to the scene said it was the work of a crazed muti killer who preyed on defenceless children in the townships. All his victims, whose ages ranged from two to six, were found without sex organs. The police knew exactly who he was, and had been working for three weeks around the clock trying to track him down. He was a thirty-year-old man from the same township, who had a young woman as his accomplice. Her role was to entice the children to lonely spots, where he butchered them and mutilated their bodies for vital parts that he used for making potent muti. The police turned and asked the onlookers if any of them knew who the dead boy was. But no one knew. They took the grisly corpse away, and it became an item on the evening news. The parents were obviously horrified when they saw their son on television. They went to the police to claim the body.

Since the crazed killer has not been arrested yet, the residents of the townships ask themselves who will die next. But if it was the crazed muti killer who murdered Noria's son, why were people angry with the Nurse when he publicly displayed his anger with the killers? Why did they say that he was giving ammunition to the enemies of the people: the government and its vigilante groups and its police? Why did they not want reporters from the newspapers to get near Noria? No, it was not the muti killer. No one would have had reservations about condemning the muti killer, and about publicizing the fact that he had struck again. Well, perhaps Noria might tell him what really happened. He will not raise the subject, though. If Noria wants to tell him, she will volunteer the information.

He alights from the taxi at the rank in the middle of the squatter camp. He walks among the shacks of cardboard, plastic, pieces of canvas and corrugated iron. He does not know where Noria lives, but he will ask. Squatter people are a close-knit community. They know one another. And by the way, he must remember that they do not like to be called squatters. 'How can we be squatters on our own land, in our own country?' they often ask. 'Squatters are those who came from across the seas and stole our land.'

The fact that he has become some kind of a spectacle does not bother him. It is his venerable costume, he knows, and is rather proud. Dirty children follow him. They dance in their tattered clothes and spontaneously compose a song about him, which they sing with derisive gusto. Mangy mongrels follow him, run alongside, sniff at him, and lead the way, while barking all the time. He ignores them all, and walks through a quagmire of dirty water and human ordure that runs through the streets of this informal settlement, as the place is politely called, looking for Noria.

3

There she is, Noria, in a rubble of charred household effects next to her burnt down shack. A lonely figure. Tall and graceful. Sharp features. Smooth, pitch-black complexion – what in the village we called poppy-seed beauty. She wears a fading red dress with white polka dots. If it was shorter and brighter Toloki would have sworn that it was the same dress that she used to wear as a little girl back in the village, dishing out pleasures to the community. She is not wearing any shoes, and is standing quite still, as if lost in thought. She hears the noise, and sees Toloki being followed by dancing children and barking dogs. 'Voetsek! Go away from here!' she shouts, and the children scamper away laughing. And the dogs flee in shame.

'They are just children, Noria.'

'They have no behaviour, those children.'

'They mean no harm.'

'They must respect their elders.'

He gives her the flowers. She smiles. He has made Noria smile.

He remembers years ago, when they were children, he was sent to the general dealer's store to buy yeast. On the way he saw a crowd of people, mostly adults, but a sprinkling of youngsters as well, standing around Noria, feasting on her laughter. Rubber Face Sehole was capering in front of her, making his famous faces, and she was laughing so much that Toloki thought her ribs would be painful. He joined the crowd. But when they saw him they shouted, 'What does this ugly child of Jwara want here? Go away, Toloki, go away!' They said that his ugly face would make Noria cry, and that this would spoil their enjoyment. He was furious at this treatment, for Noria had been his playmate when they were younger, and his face had never made her cry. And here, on this Boxing Day, he has painted a smile on Noria's sad face.

'You always knew so much about flowers, Toloki. What are these called?'

'Zinnias.'

'Thank you very much, Toloki.'

'I am sorry they don't smell nicely ... like roses.'

'It doesn't matter, Toloki. They remind me so much of the flowers you used to draw with crayons at school.'

'I could have put a dash of perfume in each one. But I had left it at my headquarters when I picked them for you.'

'They are fine the way they are.'

She tells him that she is staying with friends, until she can rebuild her shack. She explains that after killing her son, they came and petrol-bombed her home. She fled with only the clothes on her back. Toloki wonders about the identity of 'they'. She talks as though she is talking with someone who knows the facts of this tragedy. But he will be discreet. He will not ask too many questions.

She touches his hand. Her hand is warm and slightly damp. Something stirs in him. Something he has not felt in his life. Could it be pity? No. She certainly is not a pitiful figure, in spite of those plaintive eyes. She exudes strength that Toloki can definitely feel. She looks beautiful, this Noria, standing surrounded by debris, holding flowers of different colours. For the first time in his life he sees her as a woman. Not just as Noria the stuck-up bitch, daughter of That Mountain Woman. What he is feeling now is perhaps akin to what people have described as love. But then he made up his mind a long time ago that he was not capable of such feelings. They are common feelings for common people. They are taboo in his vocation, since he has cast himself in the mould of holy men in remote mountain monasteries. He has not had a personal relationship of any kind with a woman since he became a Professional Mourner. Before that, when he had just arrived in the city, he had a number of intimate friendships with many women. He has long forgotten who they were and how they looked. Perhaps he has met some of them in the cemeteries, or maybe others have passed him at the quayside as he has watched the cargo ships clumsily disembark sailors into the arms of eager prostitutes. They wouldn't remember him either, for the salty winds have ravaged his face, leaving deep gullies. There is one thing he never forgets though, by which he can identify each one of them: their moans and screams. Each steamy moan has a life of its own in his memory. These breathless sounds have sustained him through many a drought, and through them unformed children who would never know the warmth of the womb have been spewed on his hand.

'I shall help you to rebuild, Noria.'

'You are very kind, Toloki.'

'Where I live, at the docklands, there is a lot of material that you can use for rebuilding.'

'How would we get it here?'

'Plastic and canvas would not be a problem. I can carry them in a bundle in the taxi. Sheets of corrugated iron would present a problem. But one can always find a way.'

'Let us go to Shadrack's place. He might help us.'

They walk to another part of the settlement, to visit Shadrack, who is known to his friends as Bhut'Shaddy. There are two shipping containers in his yard. One serves as his house, and the other one is used as a spaza shop. Noria explains that the spaza shop, which means pseudo-shop, because it is not licensed and operates from his home, sells essential groceries such as matches, candles, paraffin and mealie-meal. It is much more expensive than the stores in town, or even in the townships, but it serves a very useful purpose for the residents of the informal settlement as it is close and convenient. Toloki notes that Noria never refers to the area as a squatter camp, or to the residents as squatters. Shadrack, Noria says, is the wealthiest member of the settlement. That is why he lives in a shipping container, instead of a makeshift shelter of newspapers, plastic, canvas and corrugated iron sheets, like the rest of the residents. He recently bought a taxi that conveys commuters between the city and the settlement. He has been blessed with good fortune because he is a good Christian, and is a member of Amadodana, the men's league of the Methodist Church.

The skorokoro van of the funeral is parked outside. From underneath it, the slight driver he saved from the wedding party bully yesterday emerges. He apologises for his dusty and greasy look, for he has been repairing his van. Then he reaches out and shakes first Noria's hand, and then Toloki's. Noria says, 'We need your help, Bhut'Shaddy. Toloki knows of a place where I can get some material to rebuild my house.' Shadrack says yes, he would like to help Noria, just as he did yesterday. But she would have to pay for the petrol. 'I do not have any money,' Noria says. 'Even yesterday the burial society paid for the petrol.' Toloki wants to know how much it will cost, and when he is told the price, he says, 'I have some money. I'll pay for the petrol.' He thinks it is rather steep, but fortunately he can afford it.

'No, I cannot take your money, Toloki. You need it too.'

'Take it, Noria. Your need is greater than mine.'

'But what will you do?'

'As long as there are funerals, I'll survive.'

Shadrack laughs. 'How do people survive on funerals?' he wants to know. Toloki explains to him, and also for Noria's benefit, the intricacies of his vocation. 'Oh, so that is how it works? I have never been to a funeral where there is a Professional Mourner,' Noria says. Shadrack wants to know why, if his services are to the benefit of humankind, the people did not want him yesterday.

'Those were people who wanted to hoard all the mourning to themselves. We do come across such greed sometimes.'

'You did not know it was Noria's child they were burying?'

'I did not know. For Noria's child, I would have mourned free of charge.'

'I did not know of your profession, Toloki. Homeboys and homegirls say you work as a beggar in the city, and you go to funerals to mooch food off the bereaved.'

'Those are people who want to dirty my name, Noria. You know that even back in the village they never liked me.'

'You will have to excuse me, people. We can talk while I repair the van. Then I can drive you to the docklands.'

He gets under his skorokoro van again, and while he is tinkering away, he tells them about the occupational hazards he encounters on a day-to-day basis while trying to improve his life, and the lives of his fellow residents. When he bought the kombi, he says, he was sure that he had cursed hunger away from the door of his house forever. But that kombi has caused him more problems than it is really worth. First he had to struggle to get a taxi licence. He had to join one of the two taxi associations that are at loggerheads with each other. He had to pay bribes to middlemen and to government officials. Then he got the licence, and thought that all his problems were over. They were not. Taxi wars erupted, with the two taxi associations fighting over routes. His driver was gunned down in one of these clashes.

As if this was not enough, his own son was killed by migrants from the hostels. They abducted him, together with three other people they picked up at random in the streets. They took them to the hostel where they set them free and asked them to run away. As they ran, the inmates fired at them to test their guns. His son, who was a matric student, and another young man were instantly killed. 'They don't know me, and they don't know my child. Why did they do it?' Noria tells him that indeed all our deaths are senseless. 'And you know, what is worse is that I am of the same ethnic group as those hostel dwellers. The tribal chief who has formed them into armies that harass innocent residents merely uses ethnicity as an excuse for his own hunger for power. I am from the same clan as this blood-soaked tribal chief.'

Toloki remembers that these arguments have come up in some of the funerals he has attended. Various Nurses, and other funeral orators, have blamed the tribal chief for all kinds of atrocities. He has concocted a non-existent threat to his people, telling them that they are at risk from other ethnic groups in the country. Whereas other leaders are trying very hard to build one free and united nation out of the various ethnic groups and races, he thinks he will reach a position of national importance by exploiting ethnicity, and by telling people of his ethnic group that if they don't fight they will be overwhelmed by other groups which are bent on dominating them, or even exterminating them. Their very existence is at stake, he teaches them. 'The rotten tribal chief is exploiting ethnicity in order to solidify his power base!' funeral orators have eruditely explained.

Some members of his ethnic group, especially those from the rural areas who still believe in the tribal authority of chiefs, follow him ardently, and have taken up arms whenever he has called upon them to do so. They are often fired up at rallies by his lyrical praise, and panegyrics, of their superiority as a group ordained by the gods; a chosen people with a history of greatness in warfare and conquest. They have internalised the version of their own identity that depicts them as having inherent aggression. When they attack the residents of squatter camps and townships, or commuters in the trains, they see themselves in the image of great warriors of the past, of whom they are descendants. Indeed the tribal chief, in his rousing speeches, has charged them with what he calls a historic responsibility to their warrior ancestors. Sometimes the police and the security forces assist them in their raids of death and destruction, because this helps to divide the people so that they remain weak and ineffective when they fight for their freedom.

There are many people from the tribal chief's clan who do not agree with him, and who are eager that the various ethnic groups should not fight, but should unite in their struggle for freedom. Shadrack is one of these people. And he says, 'You know, long before the bloody tribal chief contrived to use hostel dwellers from our ethnic group to do the dirty work for him, we, the township residents alienated ourselves from these brothers. We despised them, and said they were country bumpkins. We said they were uncivilized and unused to the ways of the city, and we did not want to associate with them. It was easy for the tribal chief to use them against us, for they were already bitter about the scorn that we were showing them.'

Noria agrees with him. She says that indeed we call them amagoduka, those whose roots are in the rural areas and who return there after their contracts in the city are finished. It was not unusual for a hostel inmate to go for a drink in the township, or to see a girlfriend, only to come back with a stab wound, or as a corpse, for the sole reason that he was a country bumpkin.

Toloki is out of his depth in this discussion. He knows there is war in the land, and has mourned at many a funeral of war casualties. But Noria seems to know more details about this whole matter than he thought possible. She talks with authority, and the man under the van seems to take her views seriously.

Shadrack says the taxi business is affected by this woeful situation. For instance, the chairman of his taxi association is deeply involved in factional violence. His luxury house, which is in the township and not in the informal settlement, is heavily guarded. He is said to support the tribal chief, and maintains close links with the police. He has recruited hostel dwellers as taxi drivers, and has kept legitimate drivers on existing routes out of work.

Taxi owners are required to pay a weekly subscription to the association, but recently they have been refusing to do so, because they have discovered that the money is being used by the chairman to purchase arms. As a result, drivers have been intimidated, several of them have been killed, and scores of taxis have been gutted. Some of the taxis are used for gunrunning in the hostels. 'I have spoken up against all this,' Shadrack says, 'and I hear rumours that they want to discipline me. Some say that my days are numbered.' He says this so casually, as if there is nothing to worry about when your days are numbered.

At last Shadrack has finished tinkering with his van.

'Your friend will sit in the back, Noria.'

'I will sit with him.'

'No ways. A lady will not sit in the back.'

'It is alright, Noria. I will sit in the back alone.'

After explaining to them exactly where the building material will be found at the docklands, Toloki climbs into the back of the van. As the van drives on the highway to the city, he watches Noria talking animatedly with Shadrack. He wonders why he had agreed to sit in the back, when there was enough space for three people in the front. No, it is not the pangs of jealousy that he feels. He is of the tradition of monks. Okay, he will admit that there is a tiny bit of curiosity in him as to what it can be that the two are talking about. And he would like to know what exactly Shadrack meant when he whispered to Noria thinking that Toloki was out of earshot, 'Your friend smells like death, Noria.' And to think he was feeling sorry for him when he heard that his days were numbered!

Shadrack drops them at Noria's site late in the afternoon. Toloki grudgingly pays him. Through Toloki's connections with dockworkers and watchmen, they were able to get plenty of building material, mostly plastic and canvas. There are sheets of iron and poles as well. And nails and ropes and pieces of wire. Noria's house is going to be beautiful, because the canvas and plastic come in all the colours of the rainbow. Noria suggests that since it is getting late, Toloki should go back to his headquarters for the night, while she guards the building material. 'I cannot leave it alone here because people will steal it,' she says.

'Are you not afraid?'

'What can they do to me? They have already killed my child.'

'I'll stay with you, Noria.'

'You have sacrificed enough, Toloki.'

'In fact, we can start building now.'

Although Noria feels that she is imposing on Toloki's kindness, they begin the construction of her shack. First they dig holes for the poles. There will be a pole at each of the four corners, and then two poles at the door. After securing the poles with small stones and with sand, they will use the remaining poles as rafters. This will be the only shack to have the luxury of rafters. Then they will put up the roof by nailing the iron sheets to the rafters. After that they will cover the sides with canvas and plastic. Thanks to Toloki's connections they have enough material to create a really elegant shack, without paper and cardboard, something much better than the one Noria had before. The finished shack will be the height of a man, which is the normal height for shacks in these informal settlements. They have reached the stage of fixing the rafters when night falls. But there is a full moon, and they continue through the night, constructing what Toloki feels is going to be a masterpiece. And of course, the moon would shine when Noria builds her house, wouldn't it?

'Your son's funeral, Noria, whose shack was that where it was held?'

'You were there? I didn't see you.'

'I only went to wash my hands, and left quickly.'

'It is the house of the chairman of the street committee.'

'Is he a homeboy?'

'No. Otherwise you would have known him.'

'Not necessarily. I left the village long time ago. And I chose not to remember the people from there.'

'How did you leave the village, Toloki? Were you looking for work?'

'No. I was running away from home.'

'Why?'

'I fought with my father.'

Fought? Actually fought with Jwara? No, Toloki explains, his father beat him up, so he ran away and vowed never to return while his father was alive. He did not have any money. He walked all the way from the village to the city. It was a long journey that took him three months.

* * *

Toloki's odyssey to a wondrous world of freedom and riches. He walked day and night, passing through farmlands and through small towns that reeked of discrimination against people of his colour. For the first time in his life, and the last time, he found himself having to beg for food. It was so demeaning to stand at a corner of a street in some nondescript town, and ask for a coin from a passer-by. He never realised it would be such a harrowing experience to be a beggar, and he vowed that he would never do it again. The experience haunts him still, even in his days as an established Professional Mourner, and it is for this reason that he will not take alms.

He walked for long distances on gravel roads. He took off his boots in order to save them from wear and tear. He hung them on his shoulders from their straps, and walked barefoot.

He was dog-tired, and his feet were swollen and numb when he entered yet another small town. It was not different from the others, for when you have been through so many country towns they all end up looking the same. He sat on the pavement, in front of a fast-food cafe. His mouth was dry with hunger. The smell of fish and chips frying in stale cooking oil made him even hungrier. It had been days since he had a morsel in his mouth, and he had terrible pains in his stomach. It was as though his empty intestines were tied in knots. If he did not get anything to eat he was surely going to die, he thought. He was not going to allow that to happen. He would rather rummage for scraps of food in the rubbish bins. Or steal. To steal is better than to beg.

A man in overalls stopped and looked at him ruthfully. Then he searched his pockets, found a coin, and gave it to him.

'Thank you, father, but I do not accept alms.'

'You do not?'

'It is true I am hungry, and if I don't eat I will die. But I do not accept charity.'

'So you'd rather die? What a stupidly proud boy!'

'I desperately need this money, father. But I insist on doing some job for you in return.'

The man in overalls laughed for a long time. Then he asked Toloki where he came from, and what he was doing in that town. Toloki told him he was on his way to the city to search for love and fortune. The man laughed again. Toloki wondered what was funny about a quest which was, in his view, so noble.

'Are all people such dreamers where you come from?'

'I do not understand why you laugh at me, father. But I am willing to do piece jobs to survive on the road.'

'I cannot offer you a job. I am just a poor labourer who lives with his old father and a lot of other labourers in a labour camp. I can introduce you to my employers who will give you a job. One of the workers left last week, and he has not been replaced yet. But don't tell them it's a piece job. They only hire people who want to work permanently. Or are you too proud to lie?'

Toloki assured him that he could lie as well as any man. The only aberration in his character was that he eschewed charity. He apologized profusely for this hang-up, and explained that he had no idea what its source was. The man bought him three fat cakes from the fast-food place, and said, 'This is not charity. You will pay me back when you receive your wages.'

They walked through the streets, while the man in overalls ran a few errands. Toloki wolfed the fat cakes, and was suddenly attacked by stomach cramps. He fell on the ground in convulsive agony.

'Hey, you can't die on me now!'

'No, it is not that, father. I ate too fast on an empty stomach.'

'Stay here. I'll go and buy you milk.'

'Thank you very much. I will pay you back. I promise I will.'

Toloki was employed as a malayisha at a mill, which meant that he loaded and unloaded bags of maize and mealie-meal. In the evenings, he slept in the watchman's shelter at the gate of the mill. He got to sleep there because he offered to help the nightwatchman guard the place, while he went to drink beer and play with women in the shebeens. Toloki's intention was to work for a few days, and then to move on as soon as he received his first weekly wages envelope.

Some days he went to visit the man who had got him the job at the labour camp, where he lived in a shack with his father. The three of them sat in front of the shack and gossiped about the neighbours, and drank beer. Sometimes they discussed the state of the nation, and the protests and demonstrations that they heard were beginning to happen in the cities. They tried to persuade Toloki to forget his quest, and keep the good job he had. Such good jobs were hard to come by, they said, and it was fortunate for him that the owner of the job had just been sacked.

'Why was he fired?'

'Oh, they accused him of stealing some bags of maize from the mill.'

His problems, Toloki was told, began one morning when he reported for duty at the milling company. The foreman ordered him to go to the manager's office, where he found policemen waiting for him. They took him away to the interrogation chambers at the police station. There they stripped him naked, and asked him to confess. But he did not know what to confess, so they beat him up. He screamed, and began to confess all the sins he could remember doing since the time he was a child. 'That's not the confession we want to hear,' the police shouted. 'We want to hear about the bags of maize you have been steal-ing to sell to one farmer whom we know very well.' The man denied any knowledge of stolen bags of maize, and his inter-rogators got angry and punched his testicles. Then they tied him to a chair and attached wires to his fingers and neck. They connected these to the electricity outlet on the wall, and the man screamed in agony and lost control of his bowels.

'Who is the farmer, and where does he stay?'

'Honest, my baas, I do not know him.'

'You sold him the maize, and yet you do not know him?'

'I never sold any maize, my baas.'

Even with all the torture they could not get any confession from this man. So they let him go. Although he was not charged with any crime, the mill refused to take him back. He lost his job, and his manhood. His wife was very angry with the police for what they did to him, and to their conjugal life.

Toloki wanted to know about the selling of maize: did it really happen? Yes, some senior workers did this from time to time. A farmer would sell a truck-load of maize to the milling company. His labourers would unload the bags at the mill. After being paid cash for the maize he would then drive back to his farm. That same afternoon, one of the drivers and the foreman at the mill would instruct the mill labourers to load a truck with the same maize. At the gate they would pretend to the security people that they were delivering mealie-meal to some wholesaler, and sign false papers. They would then take the maize back to the farmer, who would pay the driver and the foreman some money. For a long time the labourers got nothing from these transactions. But they were aware of what was happening. When they began to grumble aloud, the drivers and the foremen would buy them a lot of beer and meat after such expeditions, and they would forget about the whole thing.

'But the poor man who lost his manhood had nothing to do with the scam.'

'How can you be sure of that?'

'He was just a simple labourer. A very junior person. Only the drivers and the foremen are involved in this business. Even I, who have worked there for so many years, cannot just instruct labourers to load bags of maize onto a truck.'

'So is there nothing he can do now? Can't he go to the law?'

'Whose law? Was I not just telling you that it was the law that rendered him manless? At least in the cities we hear that they are beginning to form unions that will fight for the rights of the workers. Such ideas haven't reached us here yet.'

Toloki was convinced by his new friends to keep his job, and make his home in that country town. These companions were like family to him. He envied the cosy relationship that his new friend enjoyed with his father, and wanted to be a part of it. They were indeed more like mates, and shared everything. Theirs was the closeness of saliva to the tongue.

The father did part-time gardening jobs in a suburb where white people lived. Sometimes he came with leftovers from the

63

tables of his masters, and the three of them sat in front of the shack, and stuffed themselves with delicacies whose names they did not even know. They laughed and smoked and drank beer and danced to their own crazy off-tune songs. Toloki knew he could be happy there. For the first time in his life, he was treated like a man – even though he was only eighteen. When he shared stories of his village, people listened with genuine interest. No one laughed at his face. People were concerned with the more urgent problems of living, and with the business of creating their own happiness in the midst of penury.

One day Toloki went to visit his friends as usual. He was surprised to see a group of people standing outside the shack. Some women were weeping softly, others were wailing. He looked for the old man, and found him being comforted by other men behind the shack.

'They have killed your friend, Toloki.'

'But I saw him this morning.'

'I have just come from the hospital. He died this afternoon.'

Toloki heard how his friend was burnt to death in a deadly game he played with a white colleague. During their lunch break this white colleague sent him to fetch a gallon of petrol from the mill's petrol depot. When he came back with the petrol he found a black labourer, who was known as the white man's crony, on the floor, struggling to free himself from his white friend who had his knee on his chest. The crony later said, 'I do not know exactly how it happened, but I remember kicking the container and the man was doused with petrol all over.' As he was trying to clean his face with a piece of cloth, the white colleague jokingly said that he was going to burn him. He then struck a match and threw it at him.

The crony continued, 'The fire was so big that I was frightened. I went around screaming for help. But by the time they put out the flames and took him to hospital, it was too late. He was badly burnt.' The crony insisted that his white friend was playing. He had played such fire tricks on other workers before, including on him only the previous month. 'The same white man doused me with petrol and set me alight last month. I sustained burns, but I healed after a while. Although he is a big white baas, he is very friendly and likes to play with black labourers.'

However the man's father refused to believe that it was all a game. He said that before his son died, he had told him that the white man hated him because he was doing so well in his job. He had been a labourer for many years, serving the company with honesty and dedication, and had recently been tipped for a more senior position. The white man had conspired with the crony to kill him. They were motivated by jealousy. 'I cannot believe the many stories that are told, but I believe what my son told me,' the old man said. 'Why did the white man who burnt my son laugh at him when he was in flames? Why did he refuse to help him?' But the crony was adamant that the white colleague was merely laughing because it was a game. To him the flames were a joke. When the man screamed and ran around in pain, he thought he was dancing.

Toloki went to his friend's funeral, and solemnly listened to the Nurse explain how this our brother died. He heard of how the people led the life of birds, in fear that they would not see the next day. He heard other funeral orators talk of the wars of freedom that were beginning to take root in the cities, wars that were necessary even in that small town.

That night Toloki took his boots and hung them on his shoulders, and walked the road. He said he would not work at a place where the masters played such funless games with their servants. But first he went to say goodbye to the old man, and to pay back the money with which his deceased friend had bought him fat cakes and milk. The old man insisted that he kept the money, and wanted to give him more for provision, but Toloki said, 'Your need is greater than mine, father. I was paid only two days ago, so I still have some money.'

Toloki spent many days on the road. He walked through semi-arid lands that stretched for many miles, where the boers farmed ostriches and prickly pears. When he ran out of money, he took part-time jobs with farmers. At some places, he joined workers to harvest the prickly pears. At others, he worked for merchants who sold coal on horse carts, and who paid him only in food, after he had loaded and unloaded bags and bags of coal.

Deaths and funerals continued to dog his way throughout. For instance, in one village he found the whole community in mourning. The previous week, in a moment of mass rage, the villagers had set upon a group of ten men, beat them up, stabbed them with knives, hurled them into a shack, and set it alight. Then they had danced around the burning shack, singing and chanting about their victory over these thugs, who had been terrorizing the community for a long time. It seemed these bandits, who were roasted in a funeral pyre, had thrived on raping maidens, and robbing and murdering defenceless community members. The police were unable to take any action against these gangsters, so the members of the community had come together, and had decided to serve their own blend of justice. According to a journalist who wrote about the incident 'it was as if the killing had, in a mind-blowing instant, amputated a foul and festering limb from the soul of the community.' When Toloki got there, all the villagers were numbed by their actions. They had become prosecutors, judges and executioners. But every one of them knew that the village would forever be enshrouded by the smell of burning flesh. The community would never be the same again, and for the rest of their lives, its people would walk in a daze.

Finally, three months after leaving his village, Toloki arrived in the city.

4

The sun rises on Noria's shack. All the work has been completed, and the structure is a collage in bright sunny colours. And of bits of iron sheets, some of which shimmer in the morning rays, while others are rust-laden. It would certainly be at home in any museum of modern art. Toloki and Noria stand back, and gaze admiringly at it. First they smile, then they giggle, and finally they burst out laughing. Sudden elation overwhelms Toloki. Noria's laughter is surely regaining its old potency.

'I did not know that our hands were capable of such creation.'

'I did, Toloki. I did. You have always been good at creating beautiful things with your hands.'

'I don't believe you, Noria. You are only saying this to be nice. You know what they thought of me in the village.'

'Don't you remember the April calendar?'

'The what?'

'It is still there, Toloki. The calendar with the picture you made.'

He had forgotten about the calendar. When he won the national art competition, his colourful drawing was one of twelve that were selected for use in the following year's calendar. His was chosen for April. Even though Jwara had not shown any appreciation of the books that his son had won as a prize, Toloki hoped that he would be happy about the calendar. After all, it was going to grace the walls of homes and offices throughout the land. In April, everyone would know who Toloki was, for his name was printed just below the picture, together with the name of his school, and his age, and the class he was doing. Once more the big man from the milling company drove all the way from town to the village school to deliver a big bunch of calendars. Toloki asked for three, one each for himself, his father, and his mother. When he got home he ran excitedly to the workshop, and found his father brooding over his figurines.

'So, now you think you are better? You think you are a great creator like me?'

'I want to be like you, father. I want to create from dreams like you.'

'Don't you see, you poor boy, that you are too ugly for that? How can beautiful things come from you?'

But Toloki's mother said Jwara was jealous.

'Ha! The stupid images that you make have never appeared in any calendar. Toloki's picture will be seen all over the country.'

Jwara was so angry that he decreed that the disastrous calendar must never be seen in his house again. From that day, Toloki gave up trying to impress his father. And he gave up drawing pictures. He even – tearfully and with bitterness that gnawed at him for a long time afterwards – destroyed his precious calendar. But at his school they were proud of it, and through all the years, it was always April on the classroom wall. He is surprised to hear from Noria that to this day, after more than twenty years, it is still yellowing April at his school.

When the neighbours wake up that morning, they all come to witness the wonder that grew in the night. They marvel at the workmanship, and at how the plastic and canvas of different colours have been woven together to form patterns that seem to say something to the viewer. No one can really say what their message is, except to observe that it is a very profound one.

Toloki and Noria are working inside the shack, sweeping the floor with branches from a tree and firming it with their feet, when they hear a song outside. They walk out, and meet the singers: a group of children carrying water in small buckets and in bottles. Toloki recognises some of those who accompanied him with song and dance when he came looking for Noria yesterday.

'We have brought you water for your floor, Mother Noria.'

'Thank you, my children.'

The two creators mix soil and water to make very soft mud. Then they plaster the mud on the floor, making the geometric patterns that women make with cow dung back in the village. All the time the children sing and dance outside. At one stage they sing the song that they composed about Toloki yesterday. Noria angrily tells them that it is naughty of them to sing rude songs about adults. Toloki says, 'Let them sing, Noria. Never stifle the creativity of children.' But they are ashamed to sing the song again. Instead they sing other songs, some of which they have heard their parents, and their brothers and sisters, sing at demonstrations, and at political rallies and funerals. Soon the song becomes stronger, with the voices of adults joining in. The women of the neighbourhood, following the lead of their children, are bringing all sorts of household items to the shack. There are pots, a primus stove, a washing basin, a plastic bucket, a plate, and a spoon. There are even two old grey blankets, which are known as donkey blankets because of their colour, and a pillow. Another neighbour has brought a billycan of soured soft porridge, and steamed bread.

'We want to lend you these things, Noria. You can use them until your situation has changed for the better, when you have found yourself.'

'Thank you very much. Just leave them out there. I'll put them inside when the floor is dry.'

'You are lucky, Noria, to have neighbours like these.'

'It is our life here at the settlement, Toloki. We are like two hands that wash each other.'

By midday the performers have all left, and the creators are hungry. They sit outside the shack and eat the steamed bread, and drink the porridge from the billy. Shadrack comes and joins them. He praises their work, and thanks Toloki for helping Noria. Toloki wonders why he should take it upon himself to thank him on behalf of Noria. Where was he when he was growing up with Noria in the village? But he keeps these thoughts to himself, and gracefully accepts the man's expression of gratitude. Then Shadrack says he wants to talk privately with Noria. She stands up and they go behind the shack. Toloki can hear every word they say.

Shadrack says that he wants to return all the money she paid him for petrol. Noria wants to know why. In a voice that is hoarse with passion, he says, 'Because I have realised how much I love you, Noria. When we were in the van, and we were talking about our lives, and our dreams for our people, I realised that you were my soulmate. I think this has been growing in me for a while. I do not know why I was blind for such a long time.'

Noria thanks him for his kind words, and says that it is very flattering for her, a ragged woman of hopeless means, to be loved by such a great man as Bhut'Shaddy. Indeed the temptation is very great for her to be captivated by his honeyed tone. But unfortunately she finds it impossible to love at the moment. She advises the lovelorn man to find someone more deserving of his affection. There are many young girls – some of them are even beauty queens and others have education – who would give their right arm to be his wife. Shadrack utters an anguished scream, 'I need you, Noria. I have no one to eat my money with.'

'You need me for the wrong reasons, Bhut'Shaddy.'

'At least think about it, Noria. And please take this money.'

'I am sorry, Bhut'Shaddy, I cannot accept it.'

Noria comes back to join Toloki, who is watching a disappointed Shadrack scurry away in shame. There is a glint of satisfaction in Toloki's eyes. But then again, he realises that his glee might be premature. Perhaps Noria is playing a game with Shadrack. Women are known to play such games before accepting proposals.

'Why did you do it? You know he could make you live like a queen?'

'I do not take things from men, Toloki.'

'You do not? I thought ...'

'That was long ago, Toloki. Life has changed since then. Even you, I am going to pay you back every cent you have helped me with.'

'But I was doing it for you, Noria, because you are my home-girl, and we played together when we were children.'

'I accepted your help because I knew you were doing it from your kind heart. You did not expect anything in return. But I insist that when I have found myself, I'll pay you back.'

This is not the Noria of the village. In the village, we all knew that by the time she reached her mid-teens, she had acquired a reputation for making men happy. And in return they gave her things, which she gladly accepted. We were not sure whether it was Jwara who started her on this road. After all, she sang for him from the age of five, and he showered her with expensive presents in return.

* * *

The Noria of the village. Both she and Toloki began school in the same year. She was seven, and he was ten. He began school at a ripe old age because he had been looking after his father's small flock of sheep and goats. This was before Jwara sold the animals to Xesibe in order to concentrate on his smithy. Toloki and Noria used to walk to school together. She cut a pretty pic-ture in her khaki shirt and pitch-black gymdress, which was ironed every morning by That Mountain Woman. Unlike the gymdresses of other pupils at school, it maintained its sharp pleats, and it was not patched. Toloki, on the other hand, wore a khaki shirt and khaki shorts that were patched all over with pieces of cloth from his mother's old dresses.

Strangers would stop the two children on their way to school and comment, 'What a beautiful little girl. And look at her brother! He looks like something that has come to fetch us to the next world. Whose children are you, my children?' And Noria would give a pained squeal, 'He is not my brother!' Sometimes we would stop them when they came back from school. We would tell Toloki to run home while we detained Noria for a few moments of her laughter. She enjoyed all this attention, and as she grew older she devised ways of using it to her advantage. She knew that her influence came from her ability to give others pleasure. She could give or withhold pleasure at will, and this made her very powerful.

The older Noria grew, the further away she drifted from Toloki. She began to wear shoes, and this enhanced her feeling of self-importance. She developed other interests, and no longer played with Toloki. Even in class, ho would not see her for days on end. He would only have a glimpse of her on those afternoons when she went to sing for Jwara.

Noria would leave home in the morning wearing her beautiful gymdress, and carrying her schoolbag. When we saw a schoolbag for the first time, it belonged to Noria, of course. She would walk with the other pupils only as far as the general dealer's store, where she would disappear in one of the pit-latrines. A few minutes later she would emerge wearing the polka-dot dress that That Mountain Woman had bought her in town against Xesibe's wishes; he said that village girls of Noria's age did not wear ready-made dresses, but his words went unheard, as usual. Her face would be pale with powder, and her lips red with lipstick. Her gymdress and khaki shirt would be neatly folded in her schoolbag. She would then catch the bus to town, where she would give pleasure to bus drivers and conductors. Later, when there were mini-bus taxis that raced between the village and the town, she would ride around in these taxis, dispensing pleasure to the drivers, who would buy her gifts and flatter her. In the afternoons, she would go back to the public toilet, change into her school uniform, remove her make-up, and go home.

We saw all the things that Noria was doing, and we made the mistake of telling That Mountain Woman. She was very angry with us, and called us children of puffadders. She said we were consumed by the worms of jealousy in our sinister hearts because Noria was beautiful, and had the power to give or withhold pleasure. She went on to say that our mothers were whores who had regretfully made bad jobs of aborting us. This last one did not surprise us in the least. After all, That Mountain Woman once called her own husband, right there in front of everybody, the product of a botched abortion. Obviously it was a favourite label that she gave to people she did not like.

We did not argue with her. At that time she had begun to practise full-time as a medicine woman, and it was a credit to our wisdom that we did not challenge the razor blades in her tongue. In any case, even before she converted one of her rondavels into a consulting room where people came to be cured of ailments caused by wizards and witches, while she was still using her medical skills only for the benefit of her family and friends, we were wary of exchanging words with her.

There was a young man we used to see sauntering, or perhaps loitering, near Xesibe's homestead. He was very scrawny, and looked as if his mother had not fed him properly when he was a baby. He would walk up the pathway past Xesibe's houses, and then back again, whistling to himself. He performed this strange ritual mostly on weekends, in the evenings when the herdboys had already confined the cattle in their kraals, and were sitting around the fire roasting maize, and telling lies to one another. Sometimes Toloki would be sitting with those herdboys, reliving the time when he was one of them before he went to school, and shaping cattle and horses with the red clay that the boys brought him from the river-banks. He was much older than these boys, but he preferred their company since they did not have terrible things to say about him. They did not judge his looks as harshly as their parents did. In fact, he was their hero, as his deft hands could shape clay cattle that looked like real cattle.

Xesibe suspected the scrawny man of being a thief, who was coming to survey his big herd of cattle, with the intention of stealing some of the animals in the future. But the herdboys told him not to worry, the man posed no threat to his animals. Perhaps they knew something that he did not know. However, the fact that Noria would suddenly come alive whenever she heard the whistle did not pass unnoticed. She would put on her shoes and trip out of the house.

'Where are you going at this time of the night, Noria?'

'I am going to sing for Toloki's father, father.'

Xesibe had learnt never to complain about Noria's activities with Jwara, lest he invited his wife's scabrous tongue. That Mountain Woman, on the other hand, did not seem to notice what was happening, since she spent most of her time locked up in her consulting room, extracting evil spirits and demons from ailing patients, and administering love-potions to the lovesick and the lovelorn.

Noria did not go to sing for Jwara. Instead she went to join the scrawny young man, and together they would disappear behind the aloes. The herdboys enjoyed those moments, and would tiptoe to the aloes, and peep through the thick pointed leaves. They would then breathe heavily, and those who had already reached puberty would wet the pieces of cloth that covered their groins. They enjoyed these escapades, and whenever they saw the young man, they would become excited, for they knew that he embodied pleasures that were beyond imagination. Spying on his antics with Noria was certainly a much better experience than molesting goats in the veld. Toloki had once joined them in watching one such performance, but was so disgusted that he vomited. Since then, he was satisfied with only hearing the stories that the herdboys told about the pleasures behind the aloes, without seeing them for himself. Late in the night, when the fires had long since turned into ashes, Noria would slink back into her father's house, with pieces of dry grass stuck to the back of her head.

That Mountain Woman finally noticed that there was a scrawny young man who was paying particular attention to Noria. But at the time she did not know of the adventures behind the aloes.

'Who is he, Noria?'

'His name is Napu.'

'Where does he live? Whose child is he?'

'I do not know his parents. He lives in town.'

'What is his job?'

'He is a labourer in a brickmaking yard.'

'Did I bring you up to waste your life with mere labourers? Do you want to end up with a man who is as useless as your father?'

'But father is one of the most successful farmers in the village, with many cattle too.'

'He is still useless. And don't you answer me back. Your labourer, what does he have?'

'Nothing yet.'

'I forbid you to see him, Noria. You will be married to a teacher, or a clerk of a general dealer's store.'

A few months later we heard that Noria had run away with Napu. They were living together in a shack in the brickyard in town. That Mountain Woman was not amused. She felt that Noria had let her down. Xesibe rubbed salt into the wound, saying, 'You see, Mother of Noria, it is all your fault. Now you are paying for spoiling this child.' That Mountain Woman told him to go empty his bowels out there in the dongas, and that was the end of his I-told-you-so attitude.

We later learnt that Noria ran away because she was heavy with child. That Mountain Woman said she was very stupid to run away from home for such a trivial reason. Didn't she know that her mother had all the herbs to destroy the stomach even in the fourth month? Was she not aware of the young wives of migrants, who made mistakes in the absence of their husbands, and who came to her for assistance? If she could help strangers correct their mistakes – for a sizeable fee, of course – she would have happily helped her own daughter. Xesibe was more concerned with the shame that his family would suffer. No one from the young man's family came to negotiate lobola, and no cattle were paid to his kraal for the hand of his only daughter. Surely he was going to be a laughing stock. That Mountain Woman forbade anyone to go to town to see Noria. 'She will come back,' she said. 'I'll make her come back.'

But Noria did not come back. Although the town, which used to be two hours away by bus, was now only one hour away since the mini-bus taxis were introduced, we did not see Noria for a long time. We heard that after signing papers of marriage with her in front of a magistrate, Napu had taken her to his home village in the mountains, and had left her there with his grandmother. Napu did not have any parents, and was brought up by his grandmother. His intention was that Noria should stay there until the baby was born. His grandmother would help her nurse the baby. It did not worry them much that this was already against the custom that the first child should be born at the mother's home. Their main concern was that Noria's parents should not find her. And indeed it would have been impossible to find her in that mountain village, so far away from everywhere else.

Noria later told us of the things that happened to her in that mountain village. Napu's grandmother was a vicious woman whom Noria suspected of being a witch. Her homestead was composed of only one hovel, and her only means of survival was through the monthly allowance that Napu sent her.

One day, an old man came to visit the grandmother and stayed until late. At night, the two old fogeys mixed some herbs, boiled them, and put the water in an old rusty bathtub. Next they ordered Noria to take off her clothes, and take a bath. But she refused. They were angry with her, and cursed her, saying that she was going to suffer before she could see her child. It was late at night, and the old man did not go away. Noria decided to spread her blankets on the floor, and sleep. When they thought she was fast asleep, the grandmother stripped naked, and danced over her, chanting in some strange language. The old man just sat on the bench, and mumbled unintelligibly as if he was in a trance. Just before dawn the old man finally left, and the grandmother got into Noria's blankets and fell fast asleep.

The next morning, Noria was extremely uncomfortable in the presence of the old hag. But the grandmother was all sweet like honey, and behaved as if nothing had happened. Noria avoided her assiduously. At midday, by some stroke of good fortune and coincidence, her husband arrived. Noria was besides herself with joy. But for some strange reason that Napu could not understand, his grandmother was very angry to see him.

'What do you want here?'

'Oh, I just came, gran'ma. Just to see you and Noria.'

'To see us for what? Are you not working?'

'I got a lift from the truck of my employers. They came to deliver bricks for the construction of a general dealer's store in a village not far from here. So I thought I would come and see if the baby was born yet.'

'Well, you can see that the baby is not born yet. So what are you going to do about it?'

Noria was already into her eleventh month of pregnancy, but there was no sign of the baby. The old hag blamed Noria's own people for bewitching her. She, on the other hand, suspected the old hag, although she never before voiced her suspicions to anyone. In the presence of the grandmother, she told Napu what had happened the previous night. The old woman was shocked beyond words that an innocent-looking girl like Noria could be capable of inventing such dreadful lies about her. 'What snake is this that you have brought to my homestead, Napu, who is bent on poisoning your relations with your own grandmother who brought you up when your own parents had taken to the world, abandoning you as a baby?'

Obviously Napu did not believe Noria. But she insisted that she was going away with him. 'I am not staying another night here with your grandmother. I am going back to town with you.'

'She is not going anywhere, Napu. You cannot be controlled by a woman.'

'Oh, yes, I am going. If he does not take me with him, I'll walk the road alone. The roof of my father's house is not leaking; I'll go back there.'

Napu relented, and agreed to take Noria back to town with him. She went into the hovel, packed her few items of clothing into a pillow case, and stood outside, waiting for the road. Napu said good-bye to his grandmother, and they walked away. The grandmother shouted bitterly after them, 'You Napu, you will see the eyes of a worm! You have married that lying bitch from the lowlands! Now you are going to spend all your money on her, and I will not see even a black cent from you!'

By the thirteenth month, the lovestruck couple began to consult diviners and herbalists of all types. Where was it heard of that a woman carried a baby in her stomach for so many months? Experts mixed herbs for them, asked them to slaughter animals, and performed mysterious rituals in their brickyard shack. But still the baby refused to come. Napu finally ran out of money and could no longer afford the experts. He could not send any more money to his grandmother either, and she piled more curses on the hapless couple. Friends advised Napu to send his wife back to her home to work things out with her family. There was no doubt that That Mountain Woman had put some curse on her. When this rumour reached the ears of That Mountain Woman, she vehemently denied the accusation. 'How can I put a curse on my own daughter? In any case, I do not mix medicines that hurt people. My medicines only heal and bring good fortune, and wealth, and love, and fertility. I am not a witch. I am a doctor.'

One evening we saw Napu and Noria alighting from the bus that came from town. Noria was wearing an old donkey blanket, and she had covered her head with it so that we would not see who she was. But we knew immediately that it was Noria. Her willowy stature gave her away. She looked and walked very much like her mother in her younger days, when she first came to the village. Oh, yes, we all knew that when That Mountain Woman came to our village she was in tatters. She was strikingly beautiful, but was in rags. It was the unappreciated Xesibe who made her a person. Anyway, to go back to Noria, she walked home barefoot, as her shoes had long since worn out. Napu followed her hesitantly.

When they arrived at Noria's home, they found Xesibe and his wife eating the evening meal. When That Mountain Woman saw her daughter she wailed, 'Oh, Noria, my poor baby! You are back!' Noria threw herself into her mother's arms and wept bitterly. But Xesibe did not feel any pity for her. He said, 'Now that the world has thoroughly thrashed her, she comes back to us.' For once, That Mountain Woman did not lash at him with her tongue. Xesibe was expressing exactly her sentiments. Encouraged by this tacit consensus, he went on, 'She thinks that this world is her mother's kitchen!' Still That Mountain Woman did not lash out, but said tearfully, 'It is enough, Father of Noria, we should just be grateful that she is back.'

Then they both turned to Napu, who was just standing there like a chicken that had been soaked in water.

'And I take it this is the excuse for a man you have chosen over us?'

'He is my husband, father.'

'Husband? How many cattle did he pay?'

'I will certainly pay, sir. When I have accumulated enough money, I'll come and pay.'

'You have shown us how much you don't respect us. Your people did not even come to appease us, and to negotiate with us, after you had kidnapped our daughter.'

'I do not have any parents.'

'You mean you sprung from a stone?'

'I only have one old grandmother who brought me up. I did not mean to disrespect you, sir. I was afraid, sir, for we did you wrong. I wanted to work first, and have money, and come to make peace with you when I had lobola to pay.'

'Are you now inventing your own customs? If you knew that you were a pauper who ate lice, why did you do dirty things with my daughter?'

That Mountain Woman was more concerned with Noria's ravaged appearance. She uttered a few choice descriptive phrases. These pertained mostly to Napu's mother, and to her private parts. She did not forget to use the usual label that she stuck on people she did not like: that they were products of bungled abortions. Napu was taken aback, for in all his life he had never come across such stingingly colourful language. He immediately decided that he hated That Mountain Woman with all his heart.

'Look what this son of a viper has done to my baby!'

'It is not his fault, mother. I went with him because I loved him.'

'My own daughter wearing a donkey blanket! My daughter whose father has so many cattle he can buy all the blankets in the world! My daughter whose mother grinds and mixes medicines that can heal all humanity!'

We thought Napu would leave with his tail between his legs. But we were wrong. He became stubborn and defiant. He told them that he was not at all intimidated by That Mountain Woman, even though he was sorry that he did not go through the proper customary channels to marry their daughter. But he could see that even if he had done the right thing, Noria's parents would never have sanctioned the marriage since they had clearly shown themselves to be such snobs. Unfortunately there was nothing that they could do about it, since he, Napu, son of a nobody, had married their daughter in front of the law. Xesibe protested that his objection to the whole sorry business had nothing to do with Napu's pedigree, but had everything to do with the fact that he had disrespected them by taking their daughter without due process of custom and tradition. After all, he himself did not begin life as a wealthy man. He had been as poor as Napu, but had worked hard herding other people's animals and cultivating the land, until he accumulated his own wealth. That Mountain Woman screeched indignantly, 'Why are you on the defensive, Father of Noria? Why should we explain ourselves to this upstart? And why do you allow him to talk to me like this? Are you a man or just something that someone left behind when they squatted in the donga?'

Napu laughed mockingly in her face, and left. Xesibe was secretly pleased that there was at last someone who could stand up to his caustic wife.

Noria gave birth to a healthy baby boy after a pregnancy of fifteen months, when we had long forgotten that she was pregnant, as after a while we took her protruding stomach to be the natural order of things. In any case, we saw very little of her during that time. She stayed home and did not venture out to meet any of us at the well where we drew our water, or on the river-banks where we did our washing, or in the fields where we collected wild spinach. That Mountain Woman was very happy when the baby was finally born, and she attributed the smooth labour to her powerful medicines. She was particularly pleased with the baby's beautiful features. She claimed that he took after her own family. Despite the fact that her mother had forbidden Noria to ever contact Napu again, she sent a secret message to her husband, informing him of the birth of their son.

The next day Napu swaggered into Xesibe's homestead. Xesibe was genuinely pleased to see him, but That Mountain Woman wanted to know what the crude upstart wanted in her house.

'I have come to see my son.'

'When did you give birth to a son?'

'My wife gave birth to a son, and I have come to give him a name.'

An argument ensued. Napu had a nip of brandy in his pocket, and he kept on taking a sip from it in a very ostentatious manner. That Mountain Woman began raging in the language of the mountain people. Whenever she was extremely angry, she spoke in the language of the mountain people, and no one in the village could understand her. But it seemed that Napu was versed in this language, for he answered back. Maybe he was a mountain person too. They exchanged heated words for a long time, until That Mountain Woman got tired and broke out in our language again.

'No grandson of mine shall be named after your people.'

'He is my son, and I have decided to name him Vutha, after my own father whom I never knew!'

'My grandson shall not be dogged by misfortune just because you want to give him a stupid name that means a burning fire! Don't you know that the meanings of names are fulfilled?'

Napu insisted that his son would be called Vutha. From time to time he took a swig from his bottle, which we suspected gave him the courage to duel so bravely with That Mountain Woman. She meanwhile insisted that her grandson would be called Jealous Down, in order to spite those people who had laughed at her.

'It's an English name! My son will not have an English name!'

'That's what one would expect from an uncultured lizard like you. For your information, Jealous Down is a beautiful name. It means that the neighbours who were laughing at Noria's misfortune are now jealous because she has the most beautiful baby boy in all the village. And don't you dare imagine that you are responsible for that beauty. It comes from my side of the family!'

'Jealous Down! It does not even come from the Bible. If at least it came from the Bible, I would accept it as his church name.'

'Who told you that it does not come from the Bible? Have you read the whole Bible? Do you want to tell me that you know all the names that are in the Bible?'

The result was that Napu continued to call his son Vutha, That Mountain Woman continued to call her grandson Jealous Down, and Xesibe thought the best name would be Mistake, and proceeded to use that name at all times.

After six months, when the baby was bouncing with good health, Noria went back to live with Napu in their brickyard shack in town. Of course That Mountain Woman was against the move, but Noria was as headstrong as her mother.

'If you must go, then you are leaving Jealous Down here.'

'Oh no, I am taking Vutha with me, mother. He is my child.'

'Yes, she must take Mistake with her, Mother of Noria.'

'And who asked for your opinion, Father of Noria?'

For a while Noria lived happily with her husband. But then she discovered that he was having an affair with a neighbour. When Napu came back from work she confronted him, and they fought bitterly. She took Vutha and went back home. That Mountain Woman welcomed her back with open arms, but Xesibe said she must work things out with her husband, and must go back to build her family. He had a private heart-to-heart talk with his daughter while his wife was busy with her patients in her consulting room. He told her that he did not want a daughter who would be deemed a failure. Noria, however, said she would only go back if Napu came and apologised, and promised never to make her the object of disgrace and ridicule again. She also voiced other complaints against her husband, most of which she had been keeping to herself, in the hope that things would change for the better. The major one was that Napu was a koata, which meant that he was uncivilised and uncultured. As a result, she was finding it increasingly difficult to have anything to talk about with him.

This last complaint did not receive Xesibe's sympathy. After all, he had been called a koata for years by his wife. She ridiculed the brown blanket that he wore at all times, and said that civilised and cultured men wore jackets like the clerks at the general dealer's store. Or like the teachers at the primary school. 'But you, Father of Noria, are a koata who sleeps with his boots on!' At times, she went on to say that all his wealth was wasted on a vulgar man like him.

Napu came and begged Noria to go back home. As expected, That Mountain Woman ordered her daughter to ignore his pathetic pleas. But Xesibe's secret advice prevailed, and Noria went back to their shack in town.

Like all marriages, Noria's had its ups and downs. However, it was the down side that came to prevail. Besides the fact that Napu was a koata, and Noria had reached the stage where she never let him forget this, she became increasingly frustrated with their financial situation, which never seemed to improve. Vutha was three years old. In a year or two, they would have to send him to school. There was no doubt that even by then their situation would not have changed. Noria feared for the future. How on earth were they going to afford to send their son to school? There were fees to be paid, and one needed money to buy school uniform, without which the teachers expelled the pupils. Then one had to buy books, and make contributions to the building fund that the teachers always demanded from parents. How were they going to cope?

She could go to work. Over the years, the town had grown much bigger. Among the new places that had emerged were the hospital, the magistrate's court, the offices of the agricultural extension workers, many other buildings (most of which were government offices), and a hotel which was always full of white people who came to admire our beautiful rivers and catch catfish there. Surely she could get a job in one of these places as a sweeper, or as a woman who made tea. But Napu would not hear of it.

'My wife will not work, especially in those offices. That is where women meet men.'

'It is my fault, Napu! It is my fault that I am married to a koata!'

One night, almost at midnight, a drunken Napu came home with another woman. He ordered Noria to pack her belongings and vacate the shack.

'Where do you expect me to go at this time of the night, Napu?'

'I don't know. It is not my business where you go.'

So Noria took her few rags, and packed them in a pillow

case. She woke Vutha up, dressed him, and they both left their home. Vutha was crying.

'Where are we going, mama?'

'I don't know, my child. Ask your father.'

A neighbour gave them refuge until the next morning. Then they caught a bus back to the village. Although Noria did not have any money for the bus fare, she was well known to the bus drivers and conductors from the days when she used to spend most of her time making them happy. So they let her ride free of charge.

When Noria and her son arrived at her parents' home, she immediately sensed that something was amiss.

'Where is mother?'

'She is not here, Noria. And what do you want here anyway?'

'Napu has expelled us from his house. Where has mother gone?'

'Hospital. She was struck by illness. And since as a doctor she could not cure herself, we took her to a white doctor in town. She was immediately admitted to hospital. They say she will be there for a long time.'

We thought Xesibe would be happy without his tormentor, but again we were wrong. He claimed that he was miserable, and desperately missed his wife. Nevertheless, we could see that he enjoyed being master of his own compound. Without That Mountain Woman around, he was able to be very firm with Noria. Even though it would have been very useful to have her help in the house, he insisted that she go and find a job so as to feed her child. 'Mistake is your child, not mine. I am not giving you a single penny for his upkeep. You must go and find a job.'

Noria found a job as a sweeper in one of the government offices in town. She left the village at dawn every morning, got into a mini-bus taxi, and arrived in town two hours before the offices opened. The nightwatchman opened up for her, and she cleaned the offices. By eight, when the office workers arrived, she had finished cleaning. She was required to be around to make tea when the big bosses wanted it, or when there was an important visitor. She knocked off at three in the afternoon, and caught a taxi back to the village. This commuting would have been very expensive, and indeed would have swallowed her entire monthly salary, had it not been for the good relations that she enjoyed with the taxi drivers. She was able to travel without paying any fares.

Some days she went to the hospital to see her mother, who was slowly waning. The doctors said she had cancer of the womb. But she was always in high spirits, and her tongue had not lost its sharpness.

'Who looks after Jealous Down when you've gone to work?'

'He looks after himself.'

'He does not even go to school?'

'He's still too young, mother. He will go when he's older. And by that time I'll have enough money to pay for him.'

'Your father is a very cruel man. He has enough money to send all the children of the world to school. With a rich father like that, you don't even need to work. But I know, he is doing it to spite me.'

Vutha, meanwhile spent each day blissfully playing in the mud. He developed scabies all over his body. Xesibe said that rather than let the boy behave like a hog at home, he should go and look after the calves in the veld. Noria said that her son was not going to be anyone's herdboy. Her son would go to school instead, and receive the education that had escaped her, and become a teacher. But even as she said this, she knew that the money she was paid for sweeping the government offices was barely enough to feed them. Xesibe seemed to enjoy to see his daughter suffer.

One morning when Noria was serving tea to the big bosses, a tray laden with cups and saucers slipped from her hands and crashed to the floor. The china broke into smithereens. Noria was summarily dismissed from work.

Depressed and miserable, she went to the hospital to tell her mother of the misfortune that had befallen her. Another patient, whose bed was next to her mother's heard her story and said, 'I was only admitted yesterday, and I have been told that I am going to be here for a long time, like your mother. I was working for the Bible Society as a sweeper. Why don't you go and see them? I am sure my job is still vacant.' Noria thanked her, and immediately went to the Bible Society. She got the job.

She was much happier at the Bible Society. The women who worked there were Christians, and acted as a support group. There was one particular woman who was always expensively dressed, yet she was only a sweeper like Noria. Once Noria had got to know her, she asked, 'How do you manage to look so smart on your salary? Or do they pay you more?' The woman told her that she had other means of earning money. Sweeping at the Bible Society was only a front that gave her respectability in the eyes of her family and neighbours. The work that really paid was in the evening at the hotel. 'You can come and join me tonight and see how I work.'

That evening Noria went to the hotel with her new friend. She knew that in the village her son would probably go to sleep on an empty stomach. Xesibe could not be bothered with feeding his grandchild. In fact, in the evenings, he had taken to visiting his friends for a drink of beer that extended to the small hours of the morning. Then he sang his way home, and slept on his bed without bothering to take off his clothes or even his gumboots. Noria's hope was that Vutha would be wise enough to join the herdboys for their evening meal, which they cooked for themselves outside their hovel. One day Vutha would understand that his mother loved him very much, and that she was doing all this for him.

At the hotel, Noria learnt the art of entertaining white men who came from across the seas. In return, they bought her drinks and paid her a lot of money. Unlike her friend who introduced her to the trade, she did not find it necessary to continue working at the Bible Society. She had no need to preserve a respectable front. After all, she was earning more money in a single night than she earned in a month of drudgery either in the government offices or at the Bible Society.

She bought her son new clothes, and school uniform. She enrolled him at a private school that catered for children of his age in town. She employed a woman whose only job was to look after Vutha. In the mornings, the woman bathed him, and dressed him in his new school uniform. Then she took him to the taxi rank where he caught a mini-bus taxi to town. Our tongues began to wag about this whole suspicious affair. Did Noria think that her child was too good for the village school, where all the children of the village, including Noria herself, had gone? Anyway, whoever heard of such a young baby going to school? Where did she get all the money to spoil the brat, and to buy herself such wonderful clothes that looked like those worn by women in magazines? What kind of work was she doing? We saw her come back from town in the mornings, and leave in the late afternoons. Sometimes she only met with Vutha at the bus stop when he was coming back from school, and she was leaving for her night work. Xesibe added to the mystery when he assured us in the drinking places that none of Noria's new-found wealth came from him.

Sometimes Noria went to see her mother in hospital, accompanied by one or other of the white men she entertained. They bought fat cakes and fish and chips from a cafe and took these delicacies to That Mountain Woman. Oh, yes, the town had grown so big that it even had a cafe that sold fish and chips. That Mountain Woman would become very excited, and would address Noria in our own language so that the white men would not understand her: 'You hold tight, my child. Your father thought he could destroy you. But you are strong like your mother. I am going to get well, and when I am out of this damn hospital I am going to teach that scoundrel a bitter lesson.'

Vutha was in his second year at the private school in town, and things seemed to be working out well for everyone, until one morning Noria found the woman who looked after Vutha crying.

'It is your father, Noria.'

'What has happened? Is he dead?'

'I wish he were dead.'

The woman explained that at night, when Vutha was asleep, Xesibe tried to creep between her blankets. He wanted to take advantage of her, but she refused. He had tried it before, and when she had refused him the first time and the second time, she thought that he was going to give up. But he began to threaten her with violence, and wanted to take her valuables by force. She said she was going to pack her things and go, since she was not prepared to stay in a home where the man of the house could not control his raging lust. She was a church woman, and a married woman with a husband and children. The fact that she was in need of a job did not mean that her body was for sale.

Noria begged her not to go, and immediately went to confront her father. She found him near one of his many kraals tanning some hide with which he was going to make straps for harnessing oxen to the yoke.

'What do you think you are doing, father?'

'I am tanning leather, that's what.'

'Don't pretend you don't know what I am talking about. You tried to rape the woman who looks after Vutha.'

'Did you inherit your manners from your mother? Where did you learn to speak to your own father like that?'

'Mother was right about you all along. You have the morals of a dog. What am I going to do with Vutha if this woman leaves because of you? Are you going to look after him?'

'Now that you have a lot of money, you think you can talk to me any way you like? You have taken after your mother. Leave my house at once! Take everything of yours and leave my house!'

Noria waited for Vutha to come back from school. Once more she found herself unceremoniously packing her things, this time not into a pillow case, but into three large suitcases. When Vutha came back from school, they said good-bye to the woman who looked after him, and loaded the suitcases on a wheelbarrow. Noria pushed the heavy wheelbarrow to the bus stop, followed by a puzzled Vutha. When the bus arrived, the conductors loaded the suitcases and the wheelbarrow onto the carrier on top of the bus. The two banished passengers boarded.

Although it had been more than two years since Noria was kicked out of her marital home by her husband, she went straight back to the brickyard shack, pushing her overloaded wheelbarrow, and followed by Vutha. She kicked the door open, and found a woman cooking the evening meal on a primus stove. She could not tell whether it was the same woman for whom she was expelled from her home, or a different one. To her this was not important.

'Woman, I am back in my house. You collect your rags and go!'

'Hey, Noria, you can't just barge in …'

'You, Napu, if you value your life, you will shut up!'

The woman waited for Napu to come to her defence, but he seemed confused. He did not know what to do. There was fear in his eyes. He did not know what gave Noria the courage to act the way she was acting. Who knew what she was capable of, coming home with all that confidence and kicking up a row?

She was behaving like a raving lunatic, and no one argues with a lunatic.

'I say to you, woman, this little piece of human waste is my husband. And I have come back to my house. I say if you value your life you will leave immediately.'

The woman rushed for the door, but Noria pulled her back.

'No, you don't just leave like that. Take everything of yours.'

The poor woman packed her belongings into a pillow case and left. Napu tried to follow her, calling her name. But Noria stood at the door, and told him that he was not going anywhere.

'Let the bitch go. Your loving and loyal wife is back, Napu.'

She said these words with so much venom that Napu froze in his tracks. That night Noria did not go to work at the hotel, but slept with Vutha. In the morning she supervised her son while he washed himself, and put on his uniform. Then she showed him the road to his school, and went back to the shack. Napu sullenly left for work, and Noria remained brooding over her life. In the afternoon she went to see her mother in the hospital. That Mountain Woman had wasted away to a shadow, and was in continual agony. Still, she had faith that she was going to get well and go back home to practise her medicine, and to take her vengeance on Xesibe. Specialists had been coming from the city at least once every six months for the past two years to take a look at her. Noria decided not to tell her about Xesibe's attempted escapade with the woman who looked after Vutha.

'You have gone back to that good-for-nothing Napu? Are you out of your mind?'

'I want to give my marriage a second chance, mother.'

'A second chance? It's more like the hundredth chance. And is Napu going to allow you to continue with your work at the hotel?'

'I will take a break from my work at the hotel, and see if my marriage will work. If it does not work, I can always go back to the hotel.'

'What has come over you, Noria? How will Napu manage to support Jealous Down at an expensive school like that?'

'Vutha will have to go to an ordinary school, mother.'

'Do you call him by that terrible name of those uncultured people?'

Noria was hardened by now, and she fought back every time Napu tried to be rude or cruel to her. The bravado that he used to muster when he dealt with That Mountain Woman had fizzled out. On the days when he came home drunk, he would try to assert his manhood. But she would put him in his place. Sobriety brought sullenness. Noria told Vutha that his father was a sour-faced koata. At night she slept with her son, and Napu slept alone.

There was no direct communication between husband and wife. Noria said whatever she wanted to say through the medium of Vutha. For instance, when she was particularly fed up with Napu she would say, 'Vutha, my child, even though you have lived in this town for so many years, you are still a koata!' Or when Napu came home late, she would say, 'Vutha, my child, why do you come home drunk and so late?' And Vutha would laugh and say, 'Am I drunk, mama? Or is it Napu who is drunk?' Napu would snarl, 'I am not Napu to you. I am your father, damn it!' Sometimes the variation would go thus, 'Oh, Vutha my child, you smell like a toilet. What have you been drinking, and how many women did you sleep with?' Vutha enjoyed these little games of indirect communication. He would laugh and say, 'But, mama, it is Napu who smells like a toilet.'

Whenever Noria went to the shops and came back a little bit late, Napu would lock her out. She would knock at the door, and at the small window of the shack. Inside the shack Vutha would wreak havoc, standing by the window, throwing plates at Napu, and shouting, 'Open for my mother, you Napu! Open for my mother!' Napu would finally open the door for Noria, and after she entered the shack she would say, 'Vutha, my child, why are you so stupid? You will be a koata forever. I am only a few minutes late and you lock me out.' And Vutha would respond, 'It is Napu who is stupid, mama.'

That Mountain Woman finally died in peace at the hospital. Her funeral was an impressively big one, with many people from faraway villages coming to pay their last respects. It was only after her death that we saw how popular she had been. Noria was the Nurse at the funeral, and she moved many of those attending when she vividly described the painful road that her mother took to the other world; a road so long that it took her more than two years of pain to travel. She proudly explained that her mother did not just succumb like a coward, but fought bravely against death. She was much of a fighter in death as she had been in life. Even the specialists from the city had exclaimed in wonderment, as people who suffered from her disease did not last that long, but died within six months.

We were amazed at the dignity with which Noria carried out her heavy and heart-rending task. Some of us had objected when she was made the Nurse. We thought she was too young and inexperienced for such a grave responsibility. But we were told that it was her mother's wish that she should be the Nurse. And there she was, doing such a great job!

After the funeral Noria did not stay at her home, even though Xesibe pleaded with her to stay for a few days while certain traditional rituals were performed. She insisted on going back to her shack in town, and spoke bitter words to her father.

'You never even went to see my mother when she was in hospital.'

'I did, Noria. I did.'

'Only three times in two years! Don't deny it, you are glad she is dead.'

94

'I loved your mother, Noria.'

When she returned to her shack, however, she was dumbfounded to find it empty. Not even her own clothes were left. Noria knew immediately that Napu had finally carried out a threat he had sometimes made in his drunken moments: that one day he was going to kidnap Vutha and run away with him to a place where Noria would never find them. At the time, Noria had thought this was just an idle threat.

Noria spent days on end looking for Vutha. The police did not even try to help. They said it was a family matter. Finally, after months of searching, she gave up. By now she was a broken woman who had lost everything that meant something in her life. Still, she was absolutely convinced that one day Vutha would return to her. She decided to go to the city, to start a new life.

* * *

The stories of the past are painful. But when Toloki and Noria talk about them, they laugh. Laughter is known to heal even the deepest of wounds. Noria's laughter has the power to heal troubled souls. This afternoon, as the two of them sit in front of the shanty, exhausted from building last night's creation, and refreshing themselves with stories of the past and soured porridge, Toloki lavishly bathes his soul in her laughter.

'Well, Noria, I think I must go back to my headquarters now. My clients must be looking for me.'

'How do they usually find you, Toloki?'

'Oh, at other funerals. Those who know where I live usually leave a message in my trolley.'

'Toloki, you have helped me so much. I really don't know how to thank you enough.'

'Your laughter is enough thanks for me, Noria.'

'No, Toloki, it is not thanks enough. It would mean that we

have not grown from the days when I gave pleasure, and was paid with favours. Remember, I am going to pay you back.'

'I understand why it is important for you to pay me back, Noria. I do not object.'

'Am I going to see you again, Toloki?'

'For surely you will, Noria. I'll visit you now and then, if you don't mind, that is.'

'Of course not, I would like to see you again, silly.'

They walk together to the taxi rank in the middle of the settlement. As usual, Toloki is the centre of attraction. Heads peer inquisitively from the small doors of shanties. Passers-by gawk at them.

'Why do you prefer to use taxis? Trains are cheaper.'

'Indeed they are cheaper. But these days there is a lot of death in the trains.'

Noria laughs. She agrees that people die everyday in the trains, but jokingly asks if Toloki is afraid to die, even though his daily work involves death. Toloki returns the laughter, and says that it is true that death is his constant companion, but where one can avoid one's own death, one must do so. He has a mission in the world, that of mourning for the dead. It is imperative that he does his utmost to stay alive, so that he can fulfil his sacred trust, and mourn for the dead.

'Fortunately my mourning for the dead makes it possible for me to avoid death by using alternative transport.'

'It is a pity that the people who die every day in the trains die because they want to earn a living for their children. They have no means of using alternative transport. Thank God some have survived, and live to tell the story.'

She tells him the story of one of the residents of the settlement who escaped death by a hair's breadth only last week. He was waiting at the station when a group of men believed to be migrants from the hostels got off the train. As usual they were armed with sticks, and spears, and battleaxes, and homemade guns. He tried to board the train, but some of the men pulled him down on to the platform by his jacket. They demanded to know what ethnic group he belonged to. He told them, and it happened to be the same clan the men belonged to. They said that if he was a member of their ethnic group, then why was he not with them? Another one shouted, 'This dog is lying! He does not belong to our people. He is of the southern people who are our enemies!'

A man wielding a knife rushed towards this resident of the settlement, and was about to stab him. But the resident escaped and ran along the platform shouting for help. He ran towards a group of security guards, whom he thought would come to his rescue. To his amazement, the security guards turned on their heels and fled. The resident jumped onto the railway line and hid under a train. He clung for dear life to the axles with both hands and feet, suspending his body between the railway sleepers and the bottom of the train floor.

The migrants jumped onto the railway line to look for him. They started shoving spears and pangas underneath the train. Fortunately he was protected by the train wheels, and the weapons could not reach him.

After a while the migrants left, and the train driver came to his rescue. He told the terrified man to get into the driver's cabin, as some of the migrants were still milling about on the platform. The driver then drove the train to another station, where the resident realised for the first time that he had been stabbed in the eye.

'He is one-eyed now, but at least he is still alive.'

'He was fortunate that the white man who drove the train saved him. Other people are not that fortunate.'

Toloki tells her of another train incident, which also happened last week, where the victim was not as fortunate as this resident. A young man and his wife were in the train. She was holding their one-day-old baby. They had come from the hospital where the wife had just given birth the previous night. Three gangsters walked into the carriage and demanded that the woman give her baby to her husband and follow them. These were not migrants from hostels this time, but the very youths who live with us in the townships and in the settlements. The children we gave birth to, who have now turned against the community, and have established careers of rape and robbery.

The couple begged and pleaded. They explained that the woman had just given birth, and the baby was only a few hours old. But the gangsters showed no mercy. They insisted that the woman come with them. And she did. Not a single one of the other passengers lifted a finger to help. The next day, she was found dead in the veld. The gangsters had taken turns raping her, and had then slit her throat. Toloki knew her story because he had mourned at her funeral.

Toloki and Noria walk quietly until they reach the taxi rank. Her eyes are glassy with unshed tears.

'Mothers lose their babies, Toloki, and babies lose their mothers.'

'Death lives with us everyday. Indeed our ways of dying are our ways of living. Or should I say our ways of living are our ways of dying?'

'It works both ways. Good-bye, Toloki.'

'Good-bye, Noria.'

'Just one more thing: please take a bath. Just because your profession involves death, it doesn't mean that you need to smell like a dead rat.'

Toloki laughs good-naturedly, and promises that before he visits her again, he will take a shower at the beach. He boards the taxi with happy thoughts, and waves to Noria as it drives away.

5

Toloki wakes up early in the morning, and goes to the beach. He hopes that the gawpers will not have arrived yet, since beaches normally get crowded in the afternoons on Saturdays. He is whistling to himself, and from time to time he breaks into a jig of exhilaration. A gust of wind blows his topper away. He runs after it, performing a nifty cart-wheel that is actualised only in his imagination. He laughs aloud, until tears stream down his cheeks.

The dockworkers, the sailors and their prostitutes think that he has finally snapped. They have never seen him in this effervescent mood before. The Toloki they have known over the years has always been an incarnation of gloom and dignity.

At the beach he goes straight to the change-room, takes his clothes off, and remains in green briefs that have holes on them. Then he goes to the open showers, and scrubs his body with a stone, while the cool water slides down his back. Soon a crowd gathers around him, and they foolishly snicker and chortle. He had forgotten that during the holiday season, especially between Christmas and New Year, the beaches are always infested with rich tourists from the inland provinces. Even though he came especially early in order to avoid spectators while performing his ablutions, you really can't beat these inland spoilers. They seem to practically live on the beach.

A policeman, one of the idlers known as the beach patrol, comes and rudely tells him to clear off the beach.

'Why? What wrong have I done?'

'You are indecently dressed.'

'What about all these other people?'

'They are wearing bathing costumes, not underpants.'

'Well, mine is a bathing costume too. Who decides what is a bathing costume and what is not? Where is it written that this is not a bathing costume?'

'I don't care. When I come back, I don't want to find you here.'

He strolls away. Toloki takes his time to wash himself. He never worries about these pompous officials who like to impress the inland riff-raff by staging confrontations with him. When he finishes, he sprawls his pudgy body on the sand, and lets the morning sun dry it. Then he splashes his whole body with perfume. He is going to a funeral today. When he got home last night, there was a note on his trolley asking him to mourn at a mass funeral of five people who had died in an orgy of violence. The funeral service is due to start at about eleven. He decides to go and see Noria first, before proceeding to the cemetery.

Back in the city, he goes to furniture stores and gets as many catalogues as he can carry. He tells the salespeople that there are some customers from his village who would like to buy furniture. They would like to see the pictures first before they come to the stores to buy furniture. Of course, the salespeople don't believe him. But they don't see any harm in giving him the catalogues, which are free in any case. Then he goes to a newspaper stall, and negotiates with the owner to buy ten back issues of *Home and Garden* magazine. He buys them at only ten percent of the cover price.

He walks towards the taxi rank, and furtively picks some of the flowers that grow along the sidewalks. Then he proceeds to the pastry shop across from the taxi rank. There he buys a variety of cakes, including his favourite Swiss roll. He will buy green onions from the women who sell vegetables at a street corner just outside the pastry shop.

He gets into a taxi that will take him to the squatter camp – no, to the informal settlement. And no one turns their back on him, nor do they cover their noses. He is very pleased that he was able to get roses this time. Their scent fills the whole taxi. Noria will love these. Indeed flowers become her.

He learnt a lot about Noria yesterday. He had not really been aware of the trials she had experienced. All he knew was what had been said about her in the village – that she was just a stuck-up bitch who was spoilt. For him, she had acquired the looming stature of a wicked woman who had destroyed his father.

* * *

It is true that Noria was responsible for Jwara's downfall, and his ultimate demise. As she grew older, she developed other interests, and on many occasions failed to honour her appointments with him. Sometimes she would tell her parents that she was going to sing for Jwara. Instead, Toloki now knows, she went to charm taxi boys. Jwara's obsession could not be quenched, so he sunk deeper and deeper into depression. He could not create without Noria. Yet his dreams did not give him any respite. The strange creatures continued to visit him in his sleep, and to demand that they be recreated the next day in the form of figurines.

Often he sat in his workshop, waiting for Noria. Noria would not come. We believed that she had become too proud. Jwara sent her messages, promising her the world. The world, however, meant sweets and chocolates. Taxi boys had much more imaginative offerings.

Sometimes she went, and sang for Jwara. Then he happily created his figurines. He would come to life, be happy with the rest of his family, and treat them with love and respect. Even after Noria had gone home, and he had closed the workshop for the night, he would be lighthearted and make jokes with Toloki and with his mother. Since this was a very unnatural condition, Toloki would laugh nervously, and his mother would only scowl. Jwara would also buy delicacies such as canned corned beef and biscuits, and give these to his family. Toloki's mother would sneer mockingly, 'Ha! I can see that that stuck-up bitch Noria has given you pleasure today!'

When Noria did not come, however, Jwara became morose, and moody, and irritable. He would lose his temper for no reason at all, and slap Toloki or his mother. Toloki wished that Noria could come every day so that there would be peace and happiness in the home. He hated her when she did not come, as this inflicted pain on his family.

The last straw that broke Toloki's back came about at Easter. At this time, the Methodist Church held all-night services that were popular with us all. Even those of us who were not Christians, or who belonged to other churches, went there because their services were so lively. Their hymns, their hand-clapping, their dances, filled us all with excitement, and the stone church building, that also served as the school, would overflow with enthusiastic worshippers. It was at these services that lovers met, and unmarried teenagers made babies.

Toloki joined some boys who were sitting behind the church, drinking the brandy that they had stolen from the house of the minister, while he was busy saving people from fire and brimstone in the church. Toloki had a few sips, and soon his head was spinning around. He was not used to drinking, and the 'fire water', as the boys called the brandy, sparked in him some unnatural elation. He staggered into the church, and vigorously joined in song and dance. When the hymns stopped, and members of the congregation went to the pulpit to testify how the wondrous work of the Lord had saved them from certain damnation, Toloki's voice was heard above all other voices, shouting, 'Amen! Hallelujah! Praise the Lord!'

The hymn began again, and Toloki's dance steps gravitated towards the pulpit. He reached the pulpit, and shouted,

'Hallelujah!' We stopped the hymn and responded, 'Amen!' Then he began to preach about Christ on the cross. He invented most of the details as he went along, since the little that he knew about the Bible came from the morning readings that were done at school. His was not a family of church-goers. We couldn't care less that his story of crucifixion did not tally exactly with the version featured so prominently in the book of books. All that impressed us was that Jwara's son, whose father had never cared for the church, had finally been seized by the spirit. How could we have known that the spirit that had seized him was brandy?

He shouted, 'Ndinxaniwe! Ek is dors! Ke nyoriloe! So said the Lord Christ, hanging on the cross! I am thirsty! I am thirsty!' Then he fell down in a drunken stupor.

When he opened his eyes, it was morning, and everybody had left. His head was pounding, and he remembered only vaguely the events of the previous night. He was ashamed of himself. He went home, and drank a lot of water, which seemed to make him feel much better. Then he slept.

In the late afternoon Jwara was storming around the house, kicking everything in front of him. He was seething with rage. Toloki knew immediately that he had had an appointment with Noria, and that she had stood him up.

'What is this that I hear about you and the church?'

Toloki stutteringly tried to explain that he had merely testified as others were doing. But even before he completed a sentence, Jwara kicked him in the stomach. He fell down, vomiting blood. Jwara kicked him again and again. Toloki's mother came running, and threw herself between the two men in her life.

'What are you doing, Father of Toloki, trying to kill my child?'

'Did you not hear, Mother of Toloki? This ugly boy preached in church.'

'What if he did? What is wrong with that?'

'I don't know. People say it was a disgrace.'

'It's that stuck-up bitch Noria again, is it not? She didn't come, and you want to take it out on my child.'

That night Toloki made up his mind that he was leaving home for good. He would go to the city and find work. He told his mother, who gave him the little money that she had. In the morning, without even saying good-bye to Jwara, Toloki left his home, and his village, in search of what he later expressed to those he met on the road as love and fortune.

Throughout his long journey of many months he harboured a deep bitterness against his father. And a hatred for Noria. It was all her fault. The quarrel was not because he had disgraced his family. Jwara didn't even know what it was exactly that his son had done in church. He couldn't care less for the church. The source of all the trouble was Noria.

After all, this was not the first time that Toloki had had an altercation with the church. His first skirmish was with the Archbishop of the Apostolic Blessed Church of Holly Zion on the Mountain Top. Toloki was actually cursed by this holy prophet.

The Archbishop earned his living during the week by selling tripe and other innards of animals in a trunk fastened to the carrier of his bicycle. He rode from one homestead to another through the village, shouting, 'Mala mogodu! Amathumbo!' in his godly baritone. This simply meant that he was touting his offal, encouraging the people to buy. Some children, whose mothers had not taught them any manners, sometimes shouted at the holy man, 'Thutha mabhakethe! Tshotsha mapakethe!' What they were saying was that the Archbishop was a carrier of buckets. This emanated from the days when the holy man used to work as a nightsoil remover in town, before the Holy Spirit caught up with him, and called him to serve the Lord as the Archbishop of the Apostolic Blessed

Church of Holly Zion on the Mountain Top, which he sub-
sequently founded. The Holy Spirit had great timing, for the
Archbishop was about to lose his job in any case, since the town
was phasing out the bucket system. The municipality was
going to introduce the water cistern for the well-to-do families, and pit-latrines for the poorer ones.

On Sundays, the Archbishop conducted services in his
church, which was built of old corrugated iron sheets. Outside
there was a lopsided sign which shouted in roughly daubed letters: 'Oh come all ye faithfull to The Apostolic Blessed Church
of Holly Zion on the Mountain Top and heal yourself and your
soul and get blessed water cheap', and then the name of the
Archbishop. Toloki always wondered whenever he passed by
why 'holly' was spelt with two l's. And what the letters 'B.A.,
M.Div., D.Theol. (U.S.A.), Prophet Extraordinaire' after the
holy man's name meant.

In his church the Archbishop prayed for the sick, and dis-
pensed bottles of holy water that he himself had blessed. Since
he claimed that he could cure all sorts of illnesses, he was in
direct competition with That Mountain Woman. But there
was enough sickness to go around, and neither rival complained. However, the Archbishop acquired the reputation of
having greater expertise in extracting demons than That
Mountain Woman.

Even Noria herself, when things were not going well in her
marriage to Napu, had secretly gone to the Archbishop for his
prayers. The Archbishop asked her to confess her sins in public, and testify to the Lord. She spoke, but did not reveal everything about her life. The Archbishop said she was marked by
the devil. That Mountain Woman heard that Noria had gone
to consult her rival, and she called her daughter a traitor. But
she forgave Noria when she promised that she would never go
back again. When That Mountain Woman died, we couldn't
help noticing that there was a glint of satisfaction in the holy

man's eyes, in spite of his professed sorrow at the death of such an important member of the community.

On special days such as Easter, the Archbishop and his flock went down to the stream where he baptised new converts through immersion. The worshippers, all wearing green and white or blue and white dresses and caftans, sang to the rhythm of the drums, and danced around in circles.

On such occasions, Toloki would often be spotted on top of the hillock facing down towards the stream, mischievously throwing rocks and clods of mud at the worshippers. He would pelt them, and then hide himself. But the Archbishop would usually catch sight of him, and would curse him with everlasting misfortune in life, and everlasting fire after death.

The war between the Archbishop and Toloki was one of long standing. It had started when Toloki laughed at the holy man's flock as they were vomiting. It was part of the Easter ritual of the church to give the members of the congregation quantities of water mixed with holy herbs to induce vomiting. After the water and an enema, the worshippers would dot the hillside in a colourful display of blue, green and white, as they squatted there and threw up and emptied their bowels. This was the sacred cleansing of body and soul. Toloki and his friends enjoyed the bright spectacle, and it was the highlight of their Easter to laugh at row after row of fat buttocks decorating the hillside.

The Archbishop reported Toloki to his father, who in the presence of the holy man, talked with him strongly. The holy man himself added his heavy words, and said that it was indeed unfortunate that Toloki was fulfilling an adage that our forebears created: that glowing embers give birth to ashes. His father was an important man in the village, yet his son was as useless as cold ash. As his father spoke in serious tones, Toloki vowed in his heart that he was going to make life even more uncomfortable for the Archbishop and his flock in the village. Hence the stone-throwing incidents.

After the Archbishop had left, Toloki overheard his father telling Xesibe and a few other customers about the feud between Toloki and the church. They were all laughing and joking about it. 'They deserve what they get from these youngsters! Can you imagine grown people displaying their buttocks and doing all these strange things in front of children!' So, his father had only been pretending to be angry with him in the presence of the Archbishop! The whole fuss was just a big joke to him. This was precisely why Toloki was taken aback by Jwara's violent reaction to his Methodist Church adventure. It really had nothing to do with the church at all, and everything to do with Noria.

* * *

Toloki arrives at the settlement, carrying his bulky load of presents. He walks to the shack. This time, he is not followed by dogs and children. Perhaps they are getting used to his presence. He arrives at the shack, but Noria is not there. He sits outside and waits for her. After some time she arrives, and says that she had been at Madimbhaza's place when a child came to inform her that there was a visitor waiting for her outside her shack.

'I hope you have not been waiting for a long time.'

'No. It was not that long. Anyway, I did not tell you that I would be coming this morning.'

'It does not matter, Toloki. You are always welcome here.'

'This Madimbhaza is a friend of yours?'

'In a way, yes. It is where I do some work for the community. I will take you there one day. What are all these heavy things you are carrying?'

'I brought them for you, Noria. I brought you roses, because flowers become you like … like a second skin. Here I have magazines and catalogues with which you can decorate your walls. And here I have cakes, and green onions for myself.'

Noria thanks him, and says that he should not have gone to all that trouble on her behalf. Toloki tells her that he will help her plaster the pictures from the magazines and catalogues onto the walls in the afternoon. As for now, he has to go to a funeral, where he has been invited to mourn.

'Please let me come with you, Toloki. I want to see how you mourn.'

'You are welcome to come with me, Noria. Let us go right away. I do not want to be late.'

'I am ready. Let me just put my roses in a bottle of water first.'

At the cemetery Toloki sits on one of the five mounds, and groans, and wails, and produces other new sounds that he has recently invented especially for mass funerals with political overtones. These sounds are loosely based on chants that youths utter during political rallies. But Toloki has modified them, and added to them whines and moans that are meant to invoke sorrow and pain. He sways from side to side, particularly when the Nurse tells us the story of the death of these our brothers and sisters. He knows that Noria is watching keenly from the audience, so he gives a virtuoso performance.

'These our brothers and sisters died in a squabble over a tin of beef,' the Nurse laments. He explains that the death of these five people happened in a township that had been free from political violence for months. Then one day a man sent his wife to buy a tin of beef at a spaza shop owned by a member of the tribal chief's party. The spaza shop had run out of canned beef, so the woman bought chicken pieces instead.

When he got home her husband said he was too hungry to wait for chicken pieces. The couple returned them to the spaza shop, and asked for a refund. The shop owner refused, and an argument ensued. Blows were exchanged. The shop owner eventually took the chicken pieces back, but refused to refund the money.

The man reported the matter to his street committee, which then tried to resolve the dispute peacefully. But the shop owner was defiant, and threatened to invite the tribal chief's followers from the hostels to protect him from the street committee. The residents of the township then decided to boycott his spaza shop, and patronised other shops in the area. With his livelihood threatened, the shop owner called on the hostel dwellers to wipe out his perceived enemies in the neighbourhood. Tension mounted, and this culminated in the hostel dwellers and other supporters of the tribal chief rampaging through the township, killing student leaders, and burning down several houses belonging to community leaders.

'Since Tuesday last week five people have been killed,' said the Nurse. 'These five brothers and sisters we are laying to rest today. Many others are in hospital with serious injuries.' In the meantime, the shop owner had disappeared, and his spaza shop was now a gutted shell.

After the funeral, people come and thank Toloki, and give him some coins. One old woman says, 'I particularly invited you because I saw you at another funeral. You added an aura of sorrow and dignity that we last saw in the olden days when people knew how to mourn their dead.' Then she gives him some bank notes. Toloki puts them in his pocket without counting them. He never counts what he receives from individual funerals. However, he is still bent though on devising a fixed rate of fees for different levels of mourning, once people are used to the concept of Professional Mourner.

Noria and Toloki walk quietly back to her shack. She does not seem to know what to make of what she has just seen. Toloki was hoping for immediate praise, or at least some positive comments from her. But it seems that she chooses to reserve her opinion, almost as though she is disturbed. Oh, how eager he is to hear at least one word of approval from this powerful woman who killed his father. As they make their way back to the settlement, Toloki remembers how his father died. He had to hear it all from Nefolovhodwe, for Jwara's death began while Toloki was already on the road to the city, and was completed many years after he had reached the city.

* * *

When Noria got married to Napu and moved to town, she stopped singing for Jwara altogether. He sat in his workshop for days on end, without ever venturing out. Policemen brought horses to be shoed, but Jwara told them to go away. He was mourning the death of his creativity. He just sat in his workshop, and refused even to eat. We went to take a look at him, and found him sitting wide-eyed, staring at his figurines. We brought him food and fruit, but these remained untouched.

His wife gave up on him, and got a job doing washing for the manager of the general dealer's store. She had to earn a living, since no money was coming into the house from the smithy. After a while she no longer bothered going to the workshop, but decided to get on with her life.

We, however, continued to take him food and fruit, which kept on piling up all around him. While the food decayed, and there were worms all over the place, and a stench, he stayed intact for months on end, just staring at the figurines, and pining away. Not even once did he go out in all that time.

We finally got tired of taking the offerings to the workshop, and went about our business. But all the time we knew that Jwara was in there, lost in a trance. The workshop remained closed for many years. Sometimes we warned children, when we saw them playing outside the workshop, 'Hey you children, go and make your noise elsewhere! Don't you know that you are disturbing Jwara in his meditations?'

One day, some men who wanted to open a blacksmith business came to Toloki's mother, and offered to buy Jwara's old equipment. Toloki's mother needed the money, and didn't see the point of keeping blacksmithing equipment when it was clear to everyone that Jwara would never work as a blacksmith again. Accompanied by the men, and by other curious neighbours, she went to the workshop and opened the door. For the first time in years, light invaded the privacy of the workshop. And there was Jwara, sitting as they remembered him, but with his biltong-like flesh stuck to his bones. His bulging eyes were staring at the figurines as before. Glimmering gossamer was spun all around him, connecting his gaunt body with the walls and the roof. In front of him was a piece of paper on which he had written in a semi-literate scrawl, bequeathing his figurines to Toloki. We never knew before this that Jwara could write. In fact, we were sure that he could not write. He used to sign his papers with a cross, after Toloki or Noria had read them to him. But there it was, in his own handwriting, his last will and testament.

When Jwara was buried, no one wanted to be the Nurse. Everyone who was asked said, 'We cannot call upon ourselves the wrath of the ancestors by being witness to things we do not know. We do not know how Jwara died.'

* * *

Toloki mixes flour and sugar that he has bought from Shadrack's spaza shop, with water. He makes a paste to use for plastering the pictures from the magazines and catalogues onto the walls. The four walls are divided into different sections. On some sections, he plasters pictures of ideal kitchens. There are also pictures of lounges, of dining rooms, and of bedrooms. Then on two walls, he plasters pictures of ideal gardens and houses and swimming pools, all from the *Home and Garden* magazines. By the time he has finished, every inch of the walls is covered with bright pictures – a wallpaper of sheer luxury.

Then Toloki takes Noria's hand, and strolls with her through the grandeur. First they go to the bedroom, and she runs and throws herself on the comfortable king-size bed. Toloki hesitates, but she says, 'C'mon, Toloki. Don't be afraid. Come and sit next to me.' He sits, and the soft bedding seems to swallow them. Toloki kicks his legs up, and jumps up and down on the bed, like an excited child. Noria kneels on the bed, and also jumps up and down. They laugh like two mischievous children, and fight with the continental pillows. They play this game until they are exhausted. Then Noria sits on a stool and admires herself in the big dressing-table mirror. She makes up her face. There is a built-in radio on the head-board, and Toloki fiddles with the switch in order to get a station that plays beautiful music.

They move from the bedroom to explore the kitchen. There is a beautiful peach-coloured 'kitchen scheme', with cupboards that are fully-stocked with the ingredients for making cakes of all types, and a big fridge full of cold drinks. Some cakes are baking in the oven of the electric stove.

'You don't think the cakes in the oven are ready, Toloki?'

'They are not ready, Noria. Don't worry, a timer will call us when they are. Let's just relax and admire our beautiful home.'

They go to the lounge and stretch out on the black leather sofas. They play some more music on the stereo set, which is known as a 'music centre'. When they grow tired of the music, they laugh at idiotic American situation comedies on their wide-screen television set.

'You know, I am an outdoors type. Let's take a walk in our garden, Noria.'

'Yes, Toloki, let's go and admire our beautiful garden. You have put so much work into making it the best garden in all the land.'

They walk out of their Mediterranean-style mansion through an arbour that is painted crisp white. This is the lovely entrance that graces their private garden. Four tall pillars hoist an overhead trellis laced with Belle of Portugal roses. A bed of delphiniums, snapdragons, cosmos, and hollyhocks rolls to the foot of the arbour. Noria and Toloki take a brief rest in the wooded gazebo, blanketed by foliage and featuring a swing. Noria likes to sit on the swing, and Toloki enjoys pushing it for her.

The whole garden is a potpourri of colour, designed by expert landscape architects. Petals and scents drift above the pathways that twist and wind up the slope. The paving is made from flagstones, fitted together like a jigsaw puzzle, and curving around a bright bank of salvia, azaleas, petunias and nicotiana. There are also varieties of grasses that create a natural palette of textures, rhythm, and soft colours. There are slashing brooks and waterfalls that cascade to a collecting pool. Pools and ponds are a haven for wildlife and water plants. Besides giving the place a rugged, semi-wild look, the variety of bushes and shrubs create hiding places for Noria and Toloki when they play hide-and-seek.

It is getting late, so they must return to the house. They choose a different path made from bark and tree-trunk sections that boldly blazes the way through the flower-clustered backyard, right up to a deck of lumber with ivy and honeysuckle climbing to the rafters. The deck has an above-ground pool, and a bar. Noria and Toloki relax on the casual furniture on the deck and view the splashy fountains and frothing falls of their wonderland. When night falls, the landscape comes to shimmering life with fireflies and moonbeams – courtesy of a combination of entrance, well, tier, globe and mushroom lights. The deck glistens with spotlights and floodlights.

Back inside the house, they proceed to the dining room. Toloki covers the large oak table with a lace tablecloth. He goes to the kitchen and gets the cakes from the oven. The oven automatically switched itself off when the cakes were ready, and while Toloki and Noria were frolicking in the garden. Using some of the silverware and china that is kept in the dining-room sideboard, Toloki serves Noria with a variety of cakes. For himself, he serves only Swiss roll and green onions. They eat quietly for some time.

'It is a strange combination you are eating, is it not, Toloki?'

'It is what I eat when I really want to spoil myself. It is not the kind of food that I can afford every day.'

'But onions and cakes!'

'It is because I am austere, like the monks from faraway mountain monasteries.'

'Do they eat like that?'

'I really don't know what they eat, except for those who have faecal feeding habits – the aghori sadhu, for instance. But I had to invent a diet of my own that would mark me as an austere and ascetic votary of my own order of Professional Mourners.'

Noria does not understand what this means. But she lets it pass. She is enjoying the cakes, although in her view, which she keeps to herself, buying cakes is a waste of money. Toloki should have bought something more practical – like mealie-meal, sugar, tea, dripping, or paraffin.

After the meal, Noria clears the catalogue pages that Toloki had spread on the mud floor. They will come in handy again when she eats. Or when she sits on the floor, since her shack is devoid even of a single stool. Toloki stands up from the floor where they have both been sitting, and prepares to go. Out of the blue, Noria makes a suggestion that leaves his heart thumping at an alarmingly fast pace.

'Perhaps my ears are deceiving me, Noria.'

'I am quite serious about it, Toloki. We can live together here as homeboy and homegirl.'

'It sounds like a wonderful idea. But I am afraid. What will people say?'

'What will they say about what? We come from the same world, Toloki. Our story is the same. You are my homeboy. No one else has any business in our affair.'

'I will think about it, Noria.'

'Think seriously about it, Toloki. We must be together because we can teach each other how to live. I like you because you know how to live. I can teach you other ways of living. Today you taught me how to walk in the garden. I want to walk in that garden with you every day.'

'Yes! The garden! There is much more to it than we explored today. Many corners that we have not seen yet. I love walking in the garden with you, Noria. We shall walk in the garden every day.'

'So you'll come and live here?'

'I cannot live with anyone but myself. That's why I decided to live alone in waiting rooms. That's why I decided not to have anything to do with homeboys and homegirls. I am a monk, Noria. A man with a vocation. I mourn for the dead. I cannot stop mourning, Noria. Death continues every day. Death becomes me, it is a part of me. How will they know where to find me? How will my clients find me, Noria? I cannot live without death, Noria.'

'I cannot stop you from mourning, Toloki. It is your calling in life. And your clients will find you. It will be like relocating your business. In fact, all the deaths you mourn happen here in the settlements and in the townships, not in the docklands where you live. You will be coming home to where death is.'

His head is spinning. Does she know what she is saying, this Noria? This beautiful Noria with the soles of her feet all cracked. This intoxicating Noria, surrounded by live and dead flowers. Suddenly it somehow doesn't seem that important whether his clients find him or not. Is he doomed to be the first, and the last, Professional Mourner?

6

Toloki has nightmares that night. He is visited by strange creatures that look very much like the figurines that his father used to create. But these are made of glass. They make a terrible din, shouting his name and dancing around, all in step. Noria, also made of crystal clear and sparkling glass, appears among the creatures. She gives one sharp whistle, and the dancing and din stop abruptly. The creatures gather around her, and she feeds them glass hay. Molten glass drips from her fingers, and some of the creatures lap it. Toloki sees himself, made embarrassingly of flesh and blood, looking longingly at the scene. He wants to join Noria and her creatures. He walks towards them. But Noria rides on a glass horse that suddenly grows glass wings. It flies away with her. 'Please, Noria!' he screams, 'Don't leave me! Wait for me, Noria! Noria!' He wakes up in a sweat.

A drunk sitting on a bench a short distance away from his laughs at him. Fumes of plonk fill the waiting room.

'Who is she, ou toppie, the woman you have wet dreams about?'

'None of your business.'

'Then stop disturbing our sleep with her name.'

He takes a long swig from a bottle wrapped in brown paper, and drifts into a noisy snooze. His toothless mouth moves all the time, like a cow chewing the cud. He passes wind thunderously, which suddenly wakes him up. He thinks this is tremendously funny, so he cackles shamelessly. The stench of rotten cabbage drifts from the drunk, and hovers above Toloki. This is one of the disadvantages of his headquarters. They are a public waiting room, and sometimes, especially on weekends, they are full of inconsiderate and drunken hoboes.

'I can't stand this.'

'Stand what?'

'You farting all over the place. You are not alone here, you know.'

'You get off my case, ou toppie. It's not my fault that you have wet dreams about watchamacallit Noria.'

He laughs again. And unleashes more thunder. Toloki feels that he doesn't have to endure this. The fact that he has taken it in his stride for all the years he has lived in waiting rooms seems to escape his mind. Nor does he question why all of a sudden he can no longer tolerate it, when it has been part of his life for so long. He gets up, and pulls on his shoes. He had slept fully-dressed in what he calls his street or home clothes. He repacks all his things neatly in his supermarket trolley, and pushes it out of the waiting room. The drunk laughs and shouts after him in the mocking sing-song voice that children use when they tease each other, 'I want Noria! Give me Noria! Nye-nye, nye-nye-nye!'

Toloki walks along the highway, pushing his shopping cart. It is the middle of the night, and there are not many cars on the road. He walks unhurriedly, sometimes stopping to look at the stars. And to look back at the harbour. He is going to miss the throbbing life, the nightwatchmen, the dockworkers, the sailors and their prostitutes, even the inane grins of tourists from the inland provinces. He is making a major change in his life, and it is not clear in his mind why he is doing it.

He reaches the settlement at the crack of dawn, and stops at a bus shelter. What will Noria say when he arrives at this time of the morning? Will she not be angry with him if he wakes her up at this ungodly hour? What if she is with someone?

These unanswered questions are interrupted by a group of young men who approach him. They are the Young Tigers who patrol the streets at night, like a neighbourhood watch, protecting the people from the attacks of the migrants from the hostels, and from the police and the army. They want to know what he is doing there. He tells them that he has come to visit a friend. He has walked for many hours, all the way from the docklands, and is merely taking a rest at the bus shelter. He is shaking with fear, for he has heard what these boys, and sometimes girls, are capable of. If only he was wearing his venerable costume. They would surely show some respect for it. They look him over, and decide that he is quite harmless. 'He's just an old bum pushing his trolley,' they declare.

He immediately hastens away from their patrol zone, and goes straight to Noria's shack. He knocks, and she opens the door.

'You are up so early in the morning, Noria.'

'I am going to help Madimbhaza with the children. My God, Toloki! I wouldn't have known you in those clothes.'

'These are my civilian clothes, Noria.'

'You look strange in them. I am used to your mourning uniform.'

She does not ask what brings him here so early in the morning. It is as if she has been expecting him all along. She invites him to push his trolley into the shack, and to make himself comfortable on the floor. The donkey blankets in which she has slept are still spread on the floor, and Noria says he can sit on them. But Toloki respects the bedding of a lady, and sits on the floor, away from the blankets.

Noria tells him that Madimbhaza has many children, some of whom are physically handicapped. She goes to their shack to help her friend wash these children, and since it is Sunday today, to get them tidied up and off to church. After this she will attend a meeting of the women's organization that is trying to improve conditions for everyone at the settlement.

Toloki is welcome to come if he is interested in seeing the work she does in the community.

'I'll come next time.'

'It is fine with me. I'll be gone for most of the day. Look around and see what you can prepare for yourself.'

'I'll catch up on my sleep. I was on the road for the whole night.'

Noria leaves, and Toloki takes out his own blanket from the trolley. He spreads it on the floor and drifts into sleep. His eyes glide over the pictures on the wall. Perhaps he should cover the ceiling with pictures of furniture, and beautiful houses, and serene gardens as well. When sleeping on one's back, one should be able to take a walk in the garden. Just like in his shack when he first came to the city almost twenty years ago.

He remembers his first shack. It was in another settlement, some distance from this one. He has passed there sometimes, and has seen that the settlement has since been upgraded. Proper houses have been built, and it is now a township, and not a shanty town – as squatter camps or informal settlements were called in those days. There are streets and schools and shopping centres. But when he first came to the city, the settlement was just quagmire and shacks.

He had joined homeless people who defiantly built their shacks there against the wishes of the government. Bulldozers came and destroyed the settlement. But as soon as they left, the structures rose again. Most of the people who persisted in rebuilding now have proper houses there. Toloki would have a decent house there as well if he had not decided to follow a new path that involved sacrifice, self-denial and spiritual flagellation.

In his old shack, he had plastered pictures from magazines and newspapers on the walls, just as he has done in Noria's. The difference is that his pictures were mostly black and white, whereas Noria's are all in full colour. They make the room look much brighter, and more luxurious. Sleeping here in Noria's shack, it is as if the clock has turned back. He can see himself vividly, eighteen or so years ago, wearing spotlessly white overalls and an apron, grilling the sausages that are known as boerewors.

* * *

When Toloki arrived in the city, he had nowhere to stay. He had no job either. But he was determined not to be reduced to begging. He had heard when men talked in the village that many of those who came to the city worked as labourers at the harbour. Or on fishing trawlers. The men told stories of sea adventures, as if they themselves were sailors. They bragged of a world that Toloki had never imagined, even for a day, he would see with his own eyes, let alone be part of. So when he came to the city, he asked people how he could get to the ships.

Toloki got part-time jobs loading ships. At night he slept at the docklands, or on a bench at the railway station. He washed himself in public toilets. In those days, they did not allow people of his colour onto any of the beaches of the city, so he could not carry out his ablutions there, as he does today.

He made friends with some of the labourers, and together they went to the townships, and to the shanty towns that were mushrooming on the outskirts of the city. They visited women, and joined in drinking parties. He never really had a head for alcoholic drinks. But sometimes he would drink so that his mates would not say he was a weakling. Real men drank in those days, and it was a disgrace for anyone who professed to be a man to shun the fire waters.

It was during one of those drinking sprees that he learnt of the move by homeless people to establish another shanty town on an empty piece of land outside the city. Everybody in the shebeen was agitated. The government was refusing to give people houses. Instead, they were saying that people who had qualifying papers had to move to a new township that was more than fifty miles away from the city. How were people going to reach their places of work from fifty miles away? And yet there was land all over, close to where people worked, but it was all designated for white residential development. Most people did not even have the necessary qualifying papers. Their presence was said to be illegal, and the government was bent on sending them back to the places it had demarcated as their homelands.

The people decided that they were going to move en masse, and unilaterally take this land on the outskirts of the city, and build their shacks there. This was Toloki's opportunity to get himself a house. He joined the settlers, and allocated himself a small plot where he constructed his shack.

That was the shack that he decorated with newspapers and magazines. He was very proud of it, for it was the first property that was his alone. He was very angry when bulldozers came and destroyed it. But like the rest of the residents, he immediately rebuilt it. Sometimes state-paid vigilantes would set some of the shacks on fire, but again the shanty town was resilient.

After about a year of his doing part-time work, or piece jobs as they called them, things changed at the harbour. Times were difficult. Jobs were hard to come by. Fortunately, Toloki had saved enough money to set himself up in business.

He applied for a hawker's permit from the city council, and bought himself a trolley for grilling meat and boerewors. It was a four-wheeled trolley with a red-and-white canvas canopy hanging above it. There was a grill on one end, with a gas cylinder underneath it. In the middle were two small trays into which he put mustard and tomato sauce. At the other end was another tray for bread rolls. Mostly he put mealie-pap on this tray, as most of his customers were working people, who did not care for slight meals such as boerewors in rolls. They wanted something more solid, like pap and steak.

Toloki conducted his trade in the central business district of the city. He had many customers, some of whom would come all the way from the docklands to buy their lunch from him. He knew how to spice steak in such a way that it was suitable for the taste buds of men who were tortured by the demons of a hangover. His was the first business of that type, and he had no competition. As a result, he made a lot of money. You must remember that this was in the early days, before such street businesses became fashionable. Today there is a proliferation of them in the streets of every city in the land.

He left his shack in the mornings and caught a train to the city. Trains were still safe those days. Preachers preached about eternal damnation in them, and passengers sang hymns and clapped their hands. Souls were saved in the trains, not destroyed. The only nuisance was the pickpockets. In the city he first went to the butchery to buy meat and boerewors, and then to the bakery where he bought bread rolls. He brought the pap, which he cooked on his primus stove at home, in a big plastic bag. Then he went to the Jewish shop where he stored his trolley overnight for a small rental. He pushed his trolley to his usual corner, which the customers already knew. He wore his white overalls and an apron, and soon the air was filled with the spicy and mouth-watering aroma of grilling meat. From midday onwards, a line of hungry people would form, and his pockets bulged with profits.

He was able to furnish his shack. Soon he was going to build himself a real house. Then he was going to send for his mother in the village. At that time, Jwara had not yet completed the process of dying. He was still in his workshop staring at his figurines, but we had already given up taking offerings of fruit and food to him. Toloki did not know what was happening to

Jwara. Nor did he care. He was only interested in looking after his mother in her old age.

It was not to be. One day, business was particularly brisk. He ran out of meat. There was no one he could send to the butchery, so he chained his cart to a pole on the corner of the street for half an hour while he went to buy meat. When he came back, his cart was nowhere to be seen. He heard that city council employees had used bolt cutters to remove the chain and had taken away his trolley.

Toloki immediately reported the matter to the officer in charge of the informal trading department of the city council. He was told that his cart had been taken to the dump, and when he got there, it had already been squashed. All that was left was the front wheel. The officers of the city would not say under which regulations the action had been taken, nor who had given the instructions to demolish the cart. They said the matter was being investigated. To this day, it is still being investigated.

Toloki was reduced to cooking boerewors on a small gas cylinder cooker at the same spot where he used to park his trolley. But the customers did not come. It was not the same without the trolley.

For a while, he did not know what to do. He had some money in his post office savings book, but it was not going to last forever. And it was not enough to buy another trolley. His life had become reckless and free-spending. He had many friends who always kept him company in the afternoons and during weekends. He bought them drinks, and they swore eternal friendship. Women, too, were his ardent admirers. Not once did anyone mention his looks. He had finally found the love and fortune he had been yearning for. But when he could not maintain his life-style, the friends who loved him very much began to discover other commitments whenever he wanted their company. Women began to discover faults in him that they had not previously been aware of, and proceeded to derisively point them out.

Soon his money ran out, and he stayed in his shack all day and all night racking his brains on how to improve his lot. Then he remembered Nefolovhodwe, the furniture maker who had been his father's friend back in the village. He had been very close to Jwara and Xesibe, and the three of them used to sit together in those distant bucolic afternoons, drinking beer brewed by That Mountain Woman, and solving the problems of the world.

Nefolovhodwe used to be the poorest of the three friends. Xesibe was doing well in his farming ventures, and in animal husbandry. He was the wealthiest of the three. Jwara was not doing too badly in his smithy – until Noria destroyed him, that is. There were always horses to shoe, and farming implements to mend. Nefolovhodwe, on the other hand, was barely surviving. He had learnt carpentry skills in his youth when he worked in town. He was very good with his hands, and knew how to make chairs and tables that looked like those that were sold in stores in town, or those which were pictured in magazines. But who in the village could afford chairs and tables? Both Xesibe and Jwara had each bought a set of four chairs and a table from their friend. There were very few other men of means in the village.

Once in a while someone died, and Nefolovhodwe made a coffin for this our deceased brother or sister. His coffins were good and solid, yet quite inexpensive. At times, an order for a coffin would come all the way from town, two hours away by bus. He looked forward to the deaths of his fellow men – and women – for they put food on his pine table. But the deaths were not frequent enough.

A man from the city visited the village one day. He was one of the village people who had gone to work in the city many years ago, and had decided to live there permanently. He had come to the village only to lay a tombstone on the grave of his long-departed father, and to make a feast for the ancestors so that his path should always be covered with the smooth pebbles of success. He was drinking with the three friends when all of a sudden he said, 'You know, Nefolovhodwe, you are satisfied with living like a pauper here. But I tell you, my friend, you could make a lot of money in the city. People die like flies there, and your coffins would have a good market.'

This put some ideas in Nefolovhodwe's head. He discussed the matter with Jwara, who encouraged him to go. But he warned him to be careful not to get lost in the city. Many people went to the city and did not come back. They forgot all about their friends and relatives in the village. Nefolovhodwe promised that he would always have the village in his heart. After all, he was leaving his two best friends behind, and his wife and nine children.

In the city, Nefolovhodwe soon established himself as the best coffin maker. Like everyone else, when he first arrived, he lived in one of the squatter camps. Unlike the village, death was plentiful in the city. Every day there was a line of people wanting to buy his coffins. Then he moved to a township house. Although there was always a long waiting list for township houses, he was able to get one immediately because he had plenty of money to bribe the officials. The township house soon became too small for his needs, and for his expanding frame. He bought a house in one of the very up-market suburbs. People of his complexion were not allowed to buy houses in the suburbs in those days. He used a white man, whom he had employed as his marketing manager, to buy the house on his behalf.

The secret to Nefolovhodwe's success lay in the Nefolovhodwe Collapsible Coffin which he invented soon after his arrival in the city. The coffin could be carried by one person, like a suitcase, and it could be put together in easy steps even by a child. It was cheap enough, yet durable. The instructions that accompanied it were simple to follow, and were written in all the languages that were spoken in the city. Although it was lightweight, when it was assembled, it could carry the heaviest imaginable corpse. People came from all over – by train, by bus, by private car, and on foot – to buy the Nefolovhodwe Collapsible Coffin.

There was also the Nefolovhodwe De Luxe Special, which was a much more expensive type. Only the wealthiest people could afford it. This was also very much in demand. It was made of oak and of ebony. It had handles and hinges of gold or silver alloy. The lid had carvings of angels and other supreme beings that populate the heavens. By special order, for multi-millionaires only, some of the carvings would be made of ivory. Ivory was still easily available those days.

However, a problem arose. Smart people did not want to be buried in a Nefolovhodwe – and when people talked of a Nefolovhodwe they meant the De Luxe Special; the more popular and cheaper type was just called the Collapsible – even if they could afford it. They knew that at night, unscrupulous undertakers went to the cemetery and dug the de luxe coffin up. They wrapped the corpses in sacks, put them back in their graves, and took the coffins to sell again to other bereaved millionaires. An undertaker could sell the same coffin many times over, and no one would be the wiser. Many wealthy families thought that their loved ones were resting in peace in a Nefolovhodwe. They were not aware that they lay in a condition that was worse than that of paupers who had to be buried by prisoners. At least in pauper burials, the corpses were wrapped in strong canvas.

Nefolovhodwe knew about the digging up of his coffins, and was very disturbed by it. Although he was making millions every year, this corrupt practice affected his business and the reputation of his products. But he did not know how to stem it.

Toloki decided to go to his father's old friend. If there was anyone who could help him, it would be Nefolovhodwe. He recalled that there had been a time when Nefolovhodwe was the butt of the jokes of village children because of his poverty. He had once given a black eye to a boy who had made stupid jokes about Nefolovhodwe's tattered and gaunt appearance, and his malnourished children. 'You can't talk about my father's friend like that!' he had said, before he floored the boy with one nifty left hook. The teacher punished Toloki for fighting at school, and reported the matter to his father. Jwara never raised the issue with Toloki at all. Instead he told Nefolovhodwe about it when they were drinking That Mountain Woman's beer. Nefolovhodwe smiled when he next met Toloki and said, 'I heard what you did on my behalf when children who have no behaviour were insulting me. You are a great soldier who will grow to protect us all.' From that day on, Nefolovhodwe never skipped the opportunity to display his affection for Toloki. Even when his father referred to him as an ugly boy, Nefolovhodwe would protest.

'You don't talk like that to your own child, Jwara.'

'What would you know about it, Nef? You have never had a child like this.'

'I have nine children of my own. Some are ugly, and some are beautiful. But since they are all my children, they are all beautiful to me.'

In the city, fortune had really smiled on Nefolovhodwe. His house was surrounded by a tall security fence, which had warnings that it was electrified attached. There was a well-trimmed hedge inside the fence. Toloki went to the gate, but it was locked. He stood there for a while, not knowing what to do next. A security guard with two big Alsatians approached, and demanded to know what the hell he was doing there.

'I want to see Nefolovhodwe.'

'Just like that, eh? You want to see Nefolovhodwe?'

'I am Toloki from the village. He is my homeboy.'

The guard thought the whole thing was a joke. He laughed mockingly at Toloki.

'Your homeboy, eh? A great man like Nefolovhodwe is your homeboy? Does your homeboy want to see you too? Do you have an appointment?'

'No, I do not have an appointment. But he is my father's friend. Please tell him that Toloki, son of Jwara, wants to see him.'

The security guard hesitated for a while, then decided that he might as well just call the house and share the joke with his master. He spoke on the phone that was in the guard room by the gate, and came back to open the gate for Toloki.

'The master does not remember you. But he has a vague memory of someone called Jwara in some faraway village. He says I should let you in, but you had better have something very important to say.'

Of course the guard was lying, thought Toloki. Nefolovhodwe was not an imbecile with a short memory.

He was led by another guard across the spreading lawns, past a dozen or so German, British and American luxury cars, to the back of the double-storey mansion. They entered through the kitchen door, and Toloki was searched by another guard, before he was led through numerous passages to a big room that was expensively furnished. Nefolovhodwe, who had ballooned to ten times the size he used to be back in the village, was sitting behind a huge desk, playing with fleas. Toloki later learnt that he ran a flea circus for his relaxation. He took it very seriously, and his fleas were very good at all sorts of tricks. He believed that they would one day be skilled enough to enter an international competition.

Nefolovhodwe did not even look up as Toloki entered, but continued playing with his fleas.

'And who are you, young man?'

'I am Toloki.'

'Toloki? Who is Toloki?'

'Toloki, sir. The son of your friend, Jwara.'

'Well, I don't remember any Toloki. What do you want here?'

'I am looking for employment, sir. I thought that since you are my homeboy, and a friend of my father's, you might be able to help.'

Nefolovhodwe looked at him for the first time.

'You come and disturb my peace here at home when I am relaxing with my fleas just because you want employment? Don't you know where my office is in the city? Do you think I have time to deal with mundane matters such as people seeking employment? What do you think I employ personnel managers for?'

Toloki knew immediately that wealth had had the very strange effect of erasing from Nefolovhodwe's once sharp mind everything he used to know about his old friends back in the village. He wanted to turn his back, and leave the disgusting man with his fleas. But the pangs of hunger got the better of him, and he made up his mind that he was not going to leave that house without a job. He knelt on the floor and, with tears streaming from his eyes, pleaded with the powerful man to come to his rescue.

'I lost my business, sir. I need a job. You are the only one who can help me. Even if you don't remember me, sir, or my father, please find it in your good heart to help one miserable soul who will die without your help.'

'One miserable soul! Every time I am asked to help one miserable soul. Do you know how many miserable souls are in this city? Millions! Do you think it is Nefolovhodwe's job to feed all of them? Go to the kitchen, and tell them that I say they must give you food. Then go away from here. I do need my peace, you know.'

'It is not food I want, sir. I want a job. So that I can feed myself, and send some money to my mother. I do not want to beg, sir, or to get something for nothing. I want to work, sir, so that I can be a great man like you.'

Nefolovhodwe loved to hear that he was a great man. Although it was ridiculous to imagine that Toloki would one day be like him, he liked the part about his own greatness. Unknowingly, Toloki had pressed the right button, and he was offered a job.

'But what you'll earn depends entirely on you. I'm employing you on a commission basis. I want you to do guard duty in the cemeteries at night.'

'Guard cemeteries, sir? Who would want to steal from cemeteries?'

'You are to go to cemeteries only after funerals where a Nefolovhodwe has been used. Your task will be to hide, and wait there until someone comes to dig the coffin up. I want to catch all those undertakers who are making illicit profits from my sweat. You must admit it's an ingenious profit-making scheme, this digging up of my coffins. I should have thought of it first. If anyone is going to profit from a Nefolovhodwe, it should be Nefolovhodwe himself, don't you think so, young man?'

'Yes, sir.'

Toloki was happy that he had found a job at last. He was asked to report directly to Nefolovhodwe, and not to personnel managers in his offices in the city. He was employed directly by the great man, and was going to be paid from his own pocket, rather than from the funds of his company. This meant that he was Nefolovhodwe's personal employee. He was going to impress this big shot. He was going to catch as many thieves as possible, and earn a lot of commission in return. He pictured himself recovering from his financial difficulties, and recapturing his old life-style. But of course this time he was going to be more careful about the friends he chose. No more of the kind that loved you only when you had money. Homeboys and homegirls were the worst of the lot in this respect.

However, things were not as easy as Toloki first thought they would be. To begin with, he did not know how to find funerals where a Nefolovhodwe had been used. He went to cemeteries during the day to attend funerals, and to spy on the type of coffin used. In most cases, he found that people were using the Collapsible. The Collapsible was too cheap for anyone to dig up. He went back to report to the great man that in all the cemeteries he had visited, no one was using a Nefolovhodwe. It did not dawn on him that the sort of people who would use a Nefolovhodwe De Luxe Special would not be buried in the popular cemeteries he frequented.

'Stupid boy! You will never find a Nefolovhodwe in cemeteries in shanty towns and townships where the rabble are buried. Go to private cemeteries, ugly boy, and to church yards, foolish boy. That is where you will find a Nefolovhodwe. In the suburbs, ugly boy, in the high-class suburbs.'

Toloki was beginning to hate this new Nefolovhodwe. In many ways he reminded him of his father, Jwara.

He went to graveyards in the churches and to private cemeteries to do more spying. But they drove him away, and called him a tramp. So he stood outside the graveyard, and hoped that the coffin that was being used was a Nefolovhodwe. At night he went back and hid himself behind the trees. Months passed without his catching a single undertaker. Once a week or so he went to report back to the great man. The guard at the gate would open up for him without further ado, saying 'Come in, homeboy. Your homeboy must be expecting you.' At first Toloki thought that the guard was a homeboy. But later he realised that he was merely mocking him.

Sometimes instead of Nefolovhodwe, Toloki would find the woman who was called his wife. Toloki knew Nefolovhodwe's wife in the village, and his nine children. He had fought battles in their defence. And in defence of the honour of their now ungrateful father and husband. He refused to accept that this tall, thin girl, with straightened hair, red lips and purple eyelids, and a face that looked like that of the leupa lizard, was Nefolovhodwe's wife. She was kindhearted though, poor thing, and gave Toloki some food every time he came to report on his lack of progress in the investigations. Toloki promised himself that one day he was going to refund every cent's worth of food he had eaten at the despicable man's house.

His luck turned one night. He was waiting among marble tombstones in some posh graveyard as usual. Four men came in a van, and parked just outside the gate of the graveyard. They went to a fresh grave, and began to dig with their spades and shovels. Toloki suddenly realised that in all the briefings that he had received from the great man, there was absolutely nothing on what he should do if he caught undertakers digging the graves. He decided to confront the grave-robbers. He leapt out from his hiding place, shouting.

'At last I have got you, you dirty thieves!'

'What the hell is this? Who are you?'

'I have been looking for you for many months. I am taking you to Nefolovhodwe. You have been stealing his coffins!'

'Do you see any coffin that we have stolen here?'

'Ha! You think I am a fool. You were going to steal it.'

One man hit him hard on the head with a shovel. He fell to the ground, and spades rained down on him. The men left him for dead.

Toloki lay unconscious throughout the whole night. In the morning, he woke up with a gash on his head. His clothes were all bloody. He stood up and staggered to the grave. It was intact. He was not sure whether the thieves had continued with their digging. He went to the suburb to report to his master.

'You ugly boy, I ask you to bring me thieves, and you come with a foolish story instead. You are fired!'

Toloki had wasted months working for this man, with nothing to show for it. He was a very bitter young man. He went back to his shack and locked himself inside while he thought very hard about what to do next. Such thinking sessions usually paid off. When he had come up with the idea of selling boerewors from a trolley, it had been after he had spent days in the shack, his mind incubating new ideas. Even when he had come up with the idea of seeking Nefolovhodwe's help, it was after the same process. Well, Nefolovhodwe was a loss. But how was Toloki to know that homeboys who did well in the city developed amnesia?

Toloki observed that Nefolovhodwe had attained all his wealth through death. Death was therefore profitable. He made up his mind that he too was going to benefit from death. But unfortunately, he had no practical skill to market. Unlike Nefolovhodwe, he had no material items that he could make and sell that concerned death. But he had the saddest eyes that we had ever seen. His sad eyes were quite famous, even back in the village. We used to sing about Toloki's sorrowful eyes. Slowly he reached the decision that he was going to mourn and that people would pay him for this service. Even the fat Nefolovhodwe had told him, 'Your face is a constant reminder that we are all going to die one day.' He was going to make his face pay. After all, it was the only gift that God had given him. He was going to profit from the perpetual sadness that inhabited his eyes. The concept of a Professional Mourner was born.

The experience that he gained while working for Nefolovhodwe and looking for corrupt undertakers came in handy. He knew where and when funerals were held. He boldly approached the bereaved and told them that he was Toloki the Professional Mourner. His costume, which in those days was still new, gave him the necessary aura. He suggested that he mourn for their departed relatives for a small fee of their choice. Some people thought he was a madman or a joker. They drove him away. Others gave him some money just to get rid of him, but he mourned at their rituals all the same. He had not yet sharpened his mourning skills at that early stage. He just stood there and looked sad. It was only later that he developed certain sounds that he deemed harrowing enough to enhance the sadness and pain of the occasion.

Soon enough he learnt that it was only at poor people's funerals that he was welcome. Rich people did not want to see him at all, so he did not bother going to their funerals. When he approached poor folks, they would give him some coins, and tell him to come and mourn with them. Some, especially those who were new arrivals in the city, were puzzled. They thought that perhaps they had missed something that they ought to have been doing. Maybe it was one of the modern practices of the city to have a Professional Mourner. It was the civilised thing to do, they thought. So they engaged his services. Some believed that the presence of a Professional Mourner brought luck to their funerals. Yet there were also those who continued to see him as a nuisance.

At first, Toloki engaged in this unique profession solely for its material rewards, to profit from death like his homeboy Nefolovhodwe. But after two or three funerals, his whole outlook changed. To mourn for the dead became a spiritual vocation. As we have already seen, sometimes he saw himself in the light of monks from the Orient, and aimed to be pure like them. It was this purity that he hoped to bring to the funerals, and to share with his esteemed clients.

* * *

Noria returns at midday. She is carrying scraps of pap in a brown paper bag. She shares the food with Toloki, and tells him that this is how she has been surviving for the past few years. She helps people in the settlement with their chores. For instance, she draws water for shebeen queens. They give her food in return. Most times she helps Madimbhaza, because she has so many children, and cannot cope on her own.

'I have lived like this since I came to the city.'

'I didn't know, Noria. I could have helped.'

'You forget that I do not take things from men.'

'As a homeboy, Noria. As a brother. Not as a man.'

Noria patiently explains to him that she is not complaining about her life. She has received fulfilment from helping others. And not for one single day has she slept on an empty stomach.

* * *

Before she arrived in the city, she thought that she was going to lead a cosy life. People in the village, and in the small town where she lived in a brickmaking yard, had painted a glowing picture of life in the city. She believed that it would be possible to immerse herself in the city's glamour and allurement, and would therefore be able to forget the pain that was gnawing her as a result of losing her son. She did not want to forget the missing son, only the pain. She believed very strongly that one day Vutha would come back to her. She was going to get a job, maybe cleaning offices, or as a domestic, and build a new life. If things didn't work out, she could always fall back on her old profession of entertaining men. But on second thoughts, for Vutha's sake, she would not go back to this profession. In any case, there wouldn't be any need – the streets of the city were paved with gold and diamonds, after all.

She had a rude awakening when she arrived. There were no diamonds in the streets, nor was there gold. Only mud and open sewers. It was not like anything she had seen in her life, nor anything she had imagined. However, there was no going back. She had nothing to return to in the village.

Homegirls welcomed her. Some were doing well, working as domestics in the suburbs. Others brewed and sold beer – a practice that was illegal. But then their whole lives in the shanty towns were illegal. Word spread around that Noria had arrived in the city. She stayed with an old woman who took her under her wing because That Mountain Woman had cured her of bad spirits that had deprived her of sleep. She was still grateful, and wanted to be of assistance to the daughter of her old doctor. In return she hoped that That Mountain Woman, who was now among the revered ancestors, would look at her kindly and bless her aging life with good fortune.

Homeboys and homegirls came to the old woman's shebeen to see Noria. They cracked jokes and made funny faces, hoping that Noria would laugh and fill their miserable lives with joy. But Noria could not laugh. She tried very hard to live up to their expectations, and to make her homeboys and homegirls happy, as she had willingly done so many times back in the village, but her laughter would not come. She could only manage a strained grin; which, according to those who saw it, looked like that of someone who was constipated. It was as though the well from which the pleasant laughter flowed had run dry. Soon, everyone decided to give up, and went about with their day-to-day business.

Noria learnt the skills of brewing from the old woman. Even though her mother had been an expert brewer, Noria had never been taught the art at home. Her mother had never made her work. She, according to Xesibe, treated her daughter like an egg that would break. But in the city she worked hard. Some people from the village said that the old woman worked her like a slave. Right up until the time that she set up her own shack after the death of the old lady, she was not paid a penny, but was given food and a place to sleep instead.

Most of the people who came to drink at the old woman's shebeen were from the village. From them Noria learnt that Napu had come to the city with Vutha. As soon as her hopes were raised that at last she was going to see her son again, they looked at her with eyes that were full of pity. 'Don't you know, poor child, of the things that happened? Your son does not live anymore.' Immediately these fateful words were uttered, Noria wailed in a voice that pierced the hearts of the drinkers. The old woman was angry with them for revealing the sad news in such a tactless manner. 'Why do you think I kept quiet about it all the time? It was because I wanted to tell her myself when the time was ripe.' The drinkers apologised, explaining that they were not aware that Noria was in the dark about her son's death.

Noria learnt that Napu came to the city with Vutha. But they stayed away from everyone from the village. The home-boys and homegirls heard that Vutha was crying for his mother every day. Noria, they gossiped, had deserted her family, leaving the poor man to raise the child alone. Napu had no job, and would spend the whole day begging for money from passers-by in the city. He would sit with Vutha at a street corner, and people would throw coins into a small can that Vutha held. Most people gave money because they pitied the little boy in rags, who was pitch black with the layers and layers of filth that had accumulated on his body. Napu knew that if he went on a begging spree with Vutha, he would get a lot of money.

However, he did not spend any of this money on Vutha. When he got home – he had established a rough cardboard shelter under a lonely bridge on a disused road outside the city – he chained Vutha to a pole, and went off drinking. He went all the way to those shanty towns where he knew people from his village did not live, and crawled from shebeen to shebeen drinking, until the money was finished. Vutha would cry for

Noria and for food. But Napu would only go back to unchain him and take him to the city for more begging. The only time they had anything to eat was when some kindly people would give them scraps of food, instead of money.

One day Napu had scored a lot of money from begging. As usual, he chained Vutha to the pole under the bridge and went drinking. He was gone for many days, and forgot all about the boy. During all this time he remained in a drunken stupor, and when fellow-drinkers asked where his son was, he said he had forgotten where he had left him. The shebeen queens laughed.

'How can you forget where you have left your child?'

'I don't know. I don't have time for children. His mother will take care of him.'

'Which mother, now? Didn't you tell us that your wife died in a flood, leaving you to take care of the boy alone?'

'It's not my business. His mother will take care of him.'

The shebeen queens laughed again. They knew that the boy didn't have a mother. But they praised themselves for brewing beer that was so potent that it made Napu delirious about a wife who did not exist.

When Napu finally returned to the bridge, it was to a horrific sight. Vutha was dead, and scavenging dogs were fighting over his corpse. They had already eaten more than half of it. Napu bolted away screaming, 'They have killed my son! They have killed my son!'

He ran for many miles, without even stopping to catch his breath. He did not know where he was going. He kept on repeating that they had killed his son, and he was going to chase them until he caught them. He was going to kill them and feed them to the dogs as they had done to his son. He had taken his son away, he howled, to get even with cruel Noria. But she and her wicked mother had now murdered the poor boy. People gave way hastily as he approached. He ran until he reached the big storage dam that was part of the sewerage works of the city. He dived into the dam, and drowned.

* * *

There is a long silence after Noria has told this dreadful tale. They sit lost in sad thoughts, but Noria's eyes remain dry. Toloki remembers something from earlier days.

'You know, Noria. I used to see a dirty beggar with a small child. It was when I had just started my business grilling meat in the city. I did not know they were your husband and your son.'

'I cannot speak about my troubles any longer. Did you hear about Shadrack?'

'No.'

'He is in hospital.'

'What is he doing there?'

'I heard he was injured by the police. He is in a very serious condition. We must go and see him this afternoon.'

7

Shadrack lies on a hospital bed. There are all sorts of tubes and other contraptions jutting out of his body. He is also on a drip. Noria and Toloki stand beside the bed. He opens his eyes, and smiles wanly at them. They greet him, and tell him that they have come to see how he is doing. They have brought him some oranges and apples, since you do not go to a hospital to see a sick person without taking him or her something to eat. He thanks Noria for her kindness, but tells her that unfortunately he cannot eat any solid food. His body gets all its nourishment from the drip. He suggests, however, that they give the fruit to the old man in a neighbouring bed.

Toloki cannot help noticing that not once does Shadrack look at him. All the time he addresses himself to Noria. It is as if Toloki does not exist.

The ward is overcrowded. There are twenty beds packed into a small room, which is really meant to take only ten or so beds. Some patients are sleeping on thin mattresses under the beds. Most of those sleeping in the beds are strapped to contraptions like Shadrack's. Those who are sleeping under the beds have their legs and arms in plaster casts. All these people are casualties of the war that is raging in the land. Those who are fortunate enough to have some movement left hobble around on crutches. They silently curse the war-lords, the police and the army, or even the various political organizations, depending on whom they view as responsible for their fate. The smell of infection and methylated spirits chokes them, and leaves much of their anger unarticulated.

'What happened, Bhut'Shaddy?'

'The boers got me, Noria. They almost killed me.'

Shadrack tells them that he was ranking in his taxi last night when he was assaulted by three white men who were driving a police van. They wore khaki uniform with insignia and carried the flag of a well-known right-wing supremacist organization. This confirmed what people always said, that the right-wing supremacists have strong links with the police. The government has always denied this.

Shadrack's ordeal began when he received a message to pick up some passengers at the railway station, minutes before midnight. At the pick-up point, he parked his kombi next to the kerb, and waited. Soon after that, a police van pulled up next to him, blocking his way. The three men climbed out and rushed to his door. They jerked it open, showed him their flag, and aggressively asked if he knew what it was. He told them he was not interested. They then attacked him.

Shadrack speaks with great difficulty. He chokes with emotion.

'Maybe you can tell us the whole story when you are better, Bhut'Shaddy. Maybe talking about it makes you worse right now.'

'No, Noria. I want you to know what they did to me. They were like crazed people. They punched me. They dragged me out of my kombi and kicked me. I tried to scream, but they throttled me. Then they loaded me like a sack of potatoes into the police van.'

They lowered the van's side-blinds, and drove away with him. After about half an hour, Shadrack could feel the van reversing. It stopped and the door was opened. His kidnappers dragged him out of the van, and he was ordered to enter a dilapidated room whose door was opened just in front of him. It was freezing in the room. It was filled with naked corpses lying on the cement floor. More corpses were stacked on big shelves against the walls.

The men told him that they were going to kill him, and started assaulting him again. He stumbled over the corpses, and fell among them. When he tried to rise, the corpse of an old man was thrown onto his chest. He fell down again. One of the men grabbed him by the shoulders and ordered him to make love to a corpse of a young woman.

'I told them I'd rather die than do that with a dead person.'

'What did they say they wanted from you, Bhut'Shaddy? Why were they doing all this to you?'

'They didn't ask for anything, Noria. They were doing it just because it was a fun thing to do.'

After further assaults he was ordered out of the mortuary, and driven back to his taxi. They just dumped him there, after thanking him profusely for the good time he had given them. 'Let's do it again sometime soon,' they said, shaking his limp hand. Another taxi driver saw him lying in the road next to his old kombi. He took him to the central police station where he made a statement.

'Only a few minutes ago, just before you arrived here, I was told that one policeman had been arrested in connection with the incident.'

'That's better, Bhut'Shaddy. At least they are doing something about it.'

'Only because I have all the evidence, and full descriptions of the policemen involved. I was smart enough to contact my lawyers.'

Shadrack explains that last night, while he was writing the statement, the police officers denied that the vehicle he was describing was a police van. A Lieutenant-General even made some thinly-veiled threats, saying that if he proceeded with the matter, it would make a lot of important people angry. When important people were angry, he warned, there was no knowing what cannon they might unleash. The police could certainly not be responsible for what these angry people would do.

'Why don't you forget about the whole matter and go home to your wife and kids?'

'I am not forgetting about the matter, sir. I have been beaten up and tortured for nothing. I am laying a charge against the police. I am contacting my lawyer right away. I am contacting human rights lawyers too.'

'That's the problem with these educated ones. They think they know everything. You are a stubborn man. Don't say we didn't warn you.'

Now the police have admitted that it was indeed their van. What makes him mad is that they claim that this is an isolated incident, which does not form part of any pattern. Yet many other taxi drivers have gone through similar tortures. The experience is known as 'the hell-ride' in the taxi business. Taxi drivers who have wanted to save their lives have made love to the corpses of beautiful women with bullet wounds. Although many have survived to tell the story, some have died from the beatings. Their bodies have then been stripped naked, and left among the other corpses in the mortuary. It was sheer luck that Shadrack was able to take the registration number of the van, and then contacted his lawyers immediately. Lots of taxi drivers just consider 'the hell-ride' an occupational hazard, and never do anything about it. But with Shadrack, these sadists picked the wrong victim. He says he is going to sue the government for a lot of money.

'I tell you, I am going to be rich, Noria. They don't know what's coming to them. I am unleashing my own cannon. The hell-ride is going to make me rich. I am going to buy a brand new kombi, straight out of the box. I am going to build a big house – a real house made of bricks and roofed with tiles.'

Toloki is amazed at this man – who has ignored him since opening his eyes – surrounded by all the contraptions that speak of how close to the door of death he lies. Yet all he can think of is how rich he is going to be.

Noria tells Shadrack that they must now leave. She will come back to see him again very soon. Toloki and Noria are just about to walk out of the door of the ward when Shadrack calls Noria back. She goes back to his bed, while Toloki remains at the door, straining his ears to catch every word they say.

'Noria, is there any hope?'

'Oh, yes, Bhut'Shaddy. I am sure you'll get well again. Soon you'll be back in your business.'

'I mean about us, Noria. Is there any hope?'

'No, there is no hope. Absolutely no hope. I am very sorry about it, Bhut'Shaddy, but there is nothing I can do.'

'What do you see in him, Noria?'

'In who?'

'In Toloki. He has nothing to offer you.'

'He knows how to live, Bhut'Shaddy.'

'He stinks!'

'Not today, he doesn't. And he won't stink again.'

Toloki and Noria walk down the street to the bus stop where they will catch a bus that will drop them at the main taxi rank in the city. There they will be able to catch a taxi back to the settlement. They do not know when or how it happened, but they find themselves actually holding hands. They both pull away in embarrassment.

'I still don't understand it, Noria. You lead a difficult life. To eat you must draw water for shebeen queens. Yet you turn down a man who can change your life forever.'

'I have been chewed, Toloki. Chewed, and then spewed.'

Toloki has no idea what she means by this. But he decides not to question her further. Sometimes she talks in riddles. All that really matters is that she cares for him, as a homeboy of course. He cares for her as well, as a homegirl. Remember, he is of the stuff that venerable monks are made of.

Dusk has fallen over the settlement by the time they reach the shack. Noria opens the door, and they both enter. Noria's shack is never locked. None of the shacks in the settlement are ever locked, since there is nothing worth stealing in them. Only rich people like Shadrack lead the lives of birds that fear for their nests, and have to be on the look-out all the time to check that no one breaks into their property to steal.

Noria lights a lamp that she has made out of a half-jack bottle. There is a hole in the bottle cap, through which a wick made of an old rag is passed. She has filled the bottle with paraffin, which she got from one of the neighbours she often helps with water. They spread some papers on the floor, and sit down. It is strange for Toloki to be in a house. For many years, he has spent all his evenings in waiting rooms.

He has not slept in a house since his shack was destroyed by the vigilantes many years ago. He had just started working as a Professional Mourner at the time. Funerals were held only on Saturday or Sunday mornings those days, because death was not as prevalent then as it is at present. Today, as you know, there are funerals every day, because if the bereaved were to wait until the weekend to bury their dead, then mortuaries would overflow, and cemeteries would be overcrowded with those attending funerals. As a matter of fact, even with funerals taking place daily, the mortuaries are bursting at the seams, and the cemeteries are always jam-packed. Often there are up to ten funeral services taking place at the same time, and hymns flow into one another in unplanned but pleasant segues.

In those days, Toloki used to sit in the sun during the week, and wait for the bulldozers. Often they came during the day while people were at work. When he saw them coming, he would rush into the shack and take all his furniture out. This consisted of a single bed, two chairs, a small table on which he put his primus stove, and a bathtub. Children who remained in the other shacks would also try to save their family valuables.

Bulldozers would move in and flatten the shacks, and then triumphantly drive away. Residents would immediately rebuild, and in no time the shanty town would hum with life again. Like worker bees, the dwellers would go about their business of living.

When bulldozers failed to get rid of the shanty towns, the government devised new strategies. They recruited some of the unemployed residents, and formed them into vigilante groups. The function of these groups was to protect the people. Their method was simple, but very effective. They demanded protection money from the residents. This was collected on a weekly basis and paid to the leader of the vigilantes, who had given himself the title of Mayor. Some residents refused to pay, since they did not see why they needed to be protected by a group of layabouts who spent their days in shebeens. The shacks of those who refused to pay would mysteriously catch fire in the middle of the night. Babies sometimes died in these fires. The next day, the survivors, with the help of their neighbours, would carry out the task of rebuilding, and would make sure that they paid the protection fee in future.

Toloki was adamant that he was not going to pay any protection fee. People who were not keen to see him die advised him to stop playing the hero and pay his protection fee like all other decent citizens. One day he was summoned before the Mayor.

'I hear you are not prepared to pay the protection fee.'

'Because I don't see why I should pay it.'

'Do you think the residents who pay it are foolish? Have you ever heard of any family which diligently pays its protection fee having their house catch fire?'

Toloki laughed, and told the Mayor that he must not forget that they used to drink together when he still had his boerewors business in town.

'That is why I called you here, because I know you personally, and I don't want to see you hurt. Normally we never bother to warn people who refuse to pay. We just ignore them, and when their shacks catch fire they start running to us for protection. But in your case, I said, I know Toloki. Even though he is now doing strange things at funerals, call him here so that I can advise him like a brother that he should pay his protection fee.'

Toloki cursed under his breath, and left. The Mayor remained sitting there, with a look that clearly told of the sorrow he felt for the poor foolish man.

That night, Toloki suddenly felt hot in his sleep. When he woke up, his shack was on fire. He was only able to save his venerable costume. He stood at a distance, and watched as raging flames consumed all his dreams.

Then he walked away in a dazed state. He did not know where he was going. But his feet led him to the docklands, where he had used to work when he first came to the city, and where he had slept in waiting rooms and in toilets. He was going to establish his home in one of the quayside waiting rooms, and eschew forever the company of men. And of women.

It is strange how things don't change in these shanty towns or squatter camps or informal settlements or whatever you choose to call them. The same vigilante groups exist today, protecting the residents the same way they did eighteen or so years ago, when Toloki still had his shack. The situation is even more complicated these days, what with the tribal chief wreaking havoc with his hostel-dwelling migrants. But today people are strongly united. None of these groups are ever able to gain any lasting foothold in the settlements and in the townships. People fight back.

Toloki's eyes roam the pictures on the wall. It is a beautiful house, even if he who had a hand in its creation says so. If you don't praise yourself while you are still alive, no one else will. They will only praise you in their funeral orations when you are dead.

He wonders why Noria has invited him to stay with her. And why he agreed, turning against his vow of living the life of a hermit for the rest of his days. Things have happened too fast for his comprehension. He only met Noria on Wednesday, at the Christmas funeral of her son. And only four days later, on this memorable Sunday, he is sitting with her alone in her shack. He has moved all his worldly possession from the headquarters that have been his home for eighteen or so years.

What power does this woman have, who has dragged him into communion with live human beings, when he had vowed to dedicate all his life to the dead? What is the secret of her strength? Only four days ago she was burying her child. But here she is now, taking this tragedy in her stride. She does not carry her grief like a cross, but goes on with her life. And she says Toloki knows how to live! Only once has she mentioned the dead child, that time they fetched building materials from the docklands on Boxing Day. Who was the father of this child anyway?

She is looking at him with her penetrating eyes. Her poppy-seed skin glistens in the flickering light of the paraffin lamp. She breaks the silence.

'Why don't you ask me, Toloki?'

'Ask you what?'

'The questions that are racing through your mind.'

'You read minds, Noria. How did you know about the questions?'

'Go ahead and ask.'

'Maybe it is personal, Noria. But I want to know about your second child, the child we buried four days ago.'

'You want to know about Vutha?'

'You are confusing me, Noria. You told me that Vutha died and was eaten by dogs even before you came to the city ... perhaps fifteen or would it be seventeen years ago now ... well, the exact years don't matter. But it was many years ago. If he were alive today he would be a young man, maybe with children of his own.'

Noria smiles at the thought of grandchildren.

'I would have been a young grandmother, don't you think?'

But Toloki is not in the mood to discuss grandparenting.

'Who was the father of this new Vutha?'

He is ashamed of himself for asking the question. Issues of this nature are sensitive, especially since we know how Noria used to be free with her favours to men back in the village. But Noria is not at all angry with him. She smiles and says the child had no father.

When she first arrived in the city she had no intention of giving up her old ways. Instead, she intended to enjoy the city and all its opportunities to its fullest. But a turning point in her life came when she learnt of the death of her son, and of Napu. From that day onwards, she lost all interest in men, and her body had not, to this very day, touched that of a man. The cruelty of the world killed not only her uplifting laughter, but all human desires of the flesh.

Then one day, seven years ago, she discovered that she was pregnant. The homegirls did not believe her when she told them that she did not know how it had happened, as she had eschewed all contact with men. Although they had not seen her with any man, they believed that she had been seeing someone secretly.

'I do not expect you to believe me either, Toloki. But that is how it happened.'

'I believe you, Noria. I believe you absolutely.'

And he genuinely believes her. Noria, as Jwara used to say, is a child of the gods.

She explains that she had not slept with any man, except for the strangers that visited her in her dreams, and made love to her. Some of these dream figures began their existence on top of her as strangers, but by the time they reached their fourth ejaculation, they looked and acted like a youthful Napu. The Napu of the aloes.

Just as with her first child, Noria was pregnant for fifteen months. When the child was born, he looked exactly like the original Vutha. He even had the same birth marks. Noria decided to name him Vutha, against all the advice of the homegirls and homeboys. They said it was not wise to name a child after one who had died such a painful death. Meanings of names tended to fulfil themselves, they added. But Noria was adamant that her child would be called Vutha. So, homeboys and homegirls called him Vutha The Second, or just The Second, so as not to confuse him with his dead brother. But to Noria, he was the original Vutha who had come back to his mother.

During the few years that Vutha The Second lived with his mother, her life was blissful. She struggled to survive as before, but she wanted for nothing. When he died, he was five years old, going on for six. He had not started school yet. Noria had once taken him to the school made of shipping containers, which in fact was the only school in the settlement. But they refused to enrol him as a pupil. They said they only accepted children from the age of seven onwards. Perhaps if they had taken him at this school, he would still be alive today.

Noria's eyes are glassy with unshed tears.

'Perhaps we shouldn't talk about this, Noria. I am sorry I brought it up.'

'It is painful to remember. But we cannot pretend it did not happen.'

Toloki is longing to hear how The Second saw his death. But he will not add to Noria's sorrow by pressing the matter.

'Tomorrow I must find a funeral. My body needs to mourn.'

'I would like to go with you. Please let me go with you.'

'Was it not unsettling for you when you went with me yesterday? I did not hear you say anything about it.'

'I have not yet come to grips with it, Toloki. Please give me time to come to grips with it.'

'You know you don't have to go. I go because I cannot live without it. Not only for the money. But it is something that is in my blood. I am an addict, Noria!'

'I do want to go, Toloki. I want to participate in your world.'

Toloki is beside himself with joy when he hears this. Perhaps Noria will end up being a Professional Mourner as well. She would make an excellent Professional Mourner. And a beautiful one, too. Indeed, this would advance his long-cherished goal, that of being the founder of a noble profession.

They are both quiet for some time, lost in their thoughts. Toloki dreads the time that seems to be approaching with undignified speed, the time for sleeping. Noria crawls to the corner and gets more scraps of pap. She puts them on a piece of paper in front of Toloki, and they both eat in silence. Toloki enjoys the food, especially the slightly burnt parts that occupied the bottom of the pot when the flames licked it. It is quite a change from his cakes and green onions, or from the tinned beans which he ate when the going was not too good. Then out of the blue, Noria is distressed.

'Toloki, I am sorry about the way they treated you back in the village ... about the way we treated you.'

'It happened a long time ago, Noria. I never think about it at all.'

'You are a beautiful person, Toloki. That is why I want you to teach me how to live. And how to forgive.'

'You are the one who will teach me, Noria.'

He says this with utmost humility and modesty. His thoughts are caught by the label that Noria has given him. He has been called ugly and foolish all his life, to the extent that he has become used to these labels. But he has never been called beautiful before. It will take him time to get used to this new label. Maybe all the catastrophes that have happened in her life have affected her eyes, so that she is able to see beauty where there is none.

'Perhaps we should prepare to sleep now. If you want to pee at night, use the basin.'

'I'll go outside, Noria.'

'It can be dangerous outside. It is not like the docklands here.'

She says things so innocently, this Noria, as if it is the natural thing for a man to pee in a basin. Anyway, he knows how to hold his bladder until the next day. In the morning he will go to a public pit latrine that the residents have constructed a few hundred yards from Noria's shack.

Noria spreads her donkey blankets on the floor. Toloki spreads his on the other end of the small shack. Only a small strip of mud floor divides their separate kingdoms. She takes off her polka dot dress, and retains only her petticoat. Toloki is afraid to look at her, but a glimpse in her direction tells him that the petticoat has seen better days, and like his venerable costume, it is held together by pieces of wire and safety pins. She gets between her two donkey blankets.

'You can undress too, Toloki, and sleep. We have a very busy day tomorrow. After the funeral, I want to take you to a few places in the settlement where we do some work.'

'I always sleep with my clothes on.'

Noria laughs. It is the innocent laughter of a child. It sounds like a distant reverberation of the laughter we used to feast on when she was a little girl. Toloki cannot explain the ecstasy that suddenly overwhelms him.

'You remind me of my father. He used to sleep with his gumboots on.'

'I do take my shoes off, though, when I sleep.'

Soon Noria's breathing becomes steady and slow. Toloki shyly steals a glance at her. She sleeps in a foetal position, like all the true sons and daughters of her village. In spite of the fact that she has been in the city for so many years, she has not taken to the grotesque sleeping positions of city people. This discovery fills Toloki with admiration. And with pride. There is nothing that he wants more in the world than to wake her up, and hold her in his arms, and tell her how much he admires her, and assure her that everything will be alright. But of course he cannot do such a thing. He can't look at her sleeping posture for too long either. That would be tantamount to raping her. It would be like doing dirty things to a goddess.

8

The Nurse is a toothless old man who has seen many winters. He holds a fly-whisk made of the tail of a horse, and as he talks he uses it to whisk invisible flies from one side to another. He sways to the rhythm of his speech, working himself into an almost dance-like frenzy that leaves us panting with excitement.

'He was my age-mate, this our brother who will not see the new year,' he laments in a pained voice. 'We grew up together in a faraway village in the inland provinces. When we were little boys we looked after calves together, and when they escaped to suckle from their mothers, our buttocks received the biting pain of the whip together. When we were older we graduated together from calves to cattle, and we spent months in cattle posts in the snowy mountains. We went to the mountain school together, where we were circumcised into manhood. We went to the mines together, and dug the white man's gold that has made this land rich. Then we came to this city to work in its harbours. When we were too old to make them rich any more, we were thrown out of employment together. I tell you, my brothers and sisters, we travelled a long road with this our brother. Ours was the closeness of saliva to the tongue. And now here he lies, waiting to be laid to rest under the soil. And it is the hands of his own children that have put him in this irreversible state.'

Toloki sits on the mound. Today he floors us with a modern mourning sound that he has recently developed. He sounds like a goat that is being slaughtered.

Noria is somewhere in the crowd. She insisted on coming. They had woken up quite late, and were almost tardy for the funeral. Toloki is usually a very early riser. This morning, his eyes had opened at dawn. But he gave his back to Noria and pretended to be fast asleep. He did not know what to do once he woke up. He couldn't just sit there and ogle at Noria in her sleep. But most of all, he was ashamed of a dirty dream that had visited him in the night, leaving his perforated green underpants all wet. It was a dream about Noria. The Noria of the aloes.

After Noria had woken up, and put on her polka-dot dress, he was able to wake up too. She poured some water into a basin, took a blanket with which to cover her nakedness, and went behind the shack to wash herself. After she had finished, she came back and poured some water for him. She told him to wash himself outside. 'Wash yourself thoroughly. And don't forget to wash behind your ears,' she added. He covered himself with his blanket, pulled his pants down to his ankles, and washed his shame away. He thought of the seedy tramp who had mocked him about wet dreams in the waiting room the night before.

As he washed himself, people were passing on all sides of the shack: domestic workers rushing to catch taxis that would take them to the kitchens of their madams in the suburbs, factory workers going to the industrial areas, and pickpockets and muggers going to ply their trade in the central business district. Some of those passing by commented that it was nice that Noria had at last found herself a man. The cynics responded that for sure she had always been hiding men in her shack; no woman could survive like a nun as she pretended to do. A fat washerwoman shouted to Noria, and she responded from within the shack.

'Hey wena Noria, don't forget that this afternoon we have a meeting.'

'What would make me forget, 'Malehlohonolo?'

'Who knows? Now that you have a visitor ...'

'You are a madwoman, 'Malehlohonolo. Of course I'll attend the meeting. But you make sure that you come back from your washing early, because you must also be at the meeting.'

The fat washerwoman gave a naughty giggle, as if to say, 'Yes, Noria, I know what you were up to last night.'

Toloki was not at all bothered by the passing crowds. He is used to public ablutions. And the passers-by were not gawking at him. They were going about their business. In any case, in the settlement people generally wash themselves outside their shacks. There isn't enough room inside for ablutions.

The dream haunts Toloki as he sits on the mound, listening to the Nurse, and seasoning his oration with goatly laments. It makes something rise in the region of his groin. It is violently kicking inside his pants. Toloki bends forward as if responding to the rhythms of oration and mourning. But what he is really doing is hiding his shame. People must not see that he has disgraced his asceticism by having dirty thoughts running through his mind, and playing havoc with his venerable body.

The Nurse is now talking of how this our brother saw his death. He was a graceful patriarch who loved his family, and was a custodian of his people's customs. He was blessed with three sons. As an afterthought the Nurse adds, 'Or let me rather say, we thought it was a blessing.' And he waves in a dramatic gesture: 'But does any one of you see his sons here? No, you cannot see his sons here, my brothers and sisters, and my children. You cannot see his sons here, because none of them are here.'

He then proceeds to relate, in his histrionic manner, how the dead man's elder son died.

'Those of you who are regular in the attendance of funerals will remember that slightly more than a week ago, we buried him right here in this graveyard where many of our people sleep.' Quite a few of us mumble in agreement. We remember very well that the eldest son of the deceased was laid to rest a few days before Christmas.

Toloki does not remember that particular funeral. It is possible that he was attending other funerals at the time. With death as plentiful as it is these days, it is impossible for him to attend all funerals. All the more reason why there should be more Professional Mourners in the community.

The Nurse meanwhile continues his sorry tale.

'The son had died a normal death. Perhaps I should say an abnormal death, because he died peacefully of natural illness in his sleep. Normal deaths are those deaths that we have become accustomed to, deaths that happen everyday. They are deaths of the gun, and the knife, and torture and gore. We don't normally see people who die of illness or of old age.'

The son was buried with proper dignity. Early the next day, as was the custom, all the relatives of the deceased lined up in order to have their hair cut. The cutting of the hair is a very serious matter among some ethnic groups, the Nurse explains for the benefit of those whose customs may be different, and it is essential that it be done in the proper order. First, all the male children must have their hair cut in the order of seniority. The cutting is done by an elder in the family. After the male children, the grandmothers will have their hair cut, also in order of seniority. They are followed by the female children.

'And remember that when we talk of seniority we are not concerned with the ages of the individual children. We are talking of the seniority of the households, and of the families in relation to one another. And when we talk of children, we are talking of sons and daughters of the homesteads, irrespective of their ages. Some children have long since reached adulthood, and are fathers in their own right, but they are still children when we come to these matters. I am not trying to teach you the custom, my brothers and sisters. I am merely repeating

157

it here because it is my duty as the Nurse to tell you how this our brother saw his death.'

During the cutting of the hair, a squabble arose. The two younger brothers complained that the children of the deceased were shaved before their children. Under the usual circumstances, it would have been the proper thing to have the children of the deceased shaved before anyone else. After all, it was their father who was dead, and the two brothers were younger than the deceased. Theirs were therefore junior homesteads. But the circumstances of this case were that the deceased had made the children in question with a mistress, and not with a legally married wife. The two younger brothers therefore felt it was a crime that their children should be shaved after the children of a mistress.

'They blamed their father, my friend the patriarch we are burying today, for allowing the scandal to happen. As an elder, and a custodian of the customs, he should not have allowed the children of a mistress to be shaved before their legitimate children. So, they beat him up with sticks. I was called from my shack by the screams of the women. When I arrived there, one of the boys even had a gun, and was surely going to use it on his father. I told him to shoot me as well, if he was going to shoot my friend. I tell you, my brothers and sisters, and my children, I nearly joined my age-mate in death. But it seems that my ancestors were too strong for these evil boys. They stopped beating up their father, and went into the house to carry on with the cutting of the hair according to how they saw fit.'

The old man ran up and down the whole settlement, trying to find transport to take his friend to hospital. But the cars he saw in the streets all refused to stop for him.

'Shadrack is the person who usually helps us with transport at times like these. But he was away ranking in the city. You know that he does the ranking himself now, as they killed all his drivers. They killed his son too. And this very day, my brothers and sisters, he is lying in hospital because the upholders of the law tried to finish him. They do not want to see anyone helping his own people. I am told that the day before yesterday he miraculously escaped death. I have not been to see him yet. After this funeral I intend to go to the hospital to visit him. Anyway, I am still telling you how this our brother saw his death.

'I waited outside Shadrack's spaza shop, until it was late in the evening. He arrived at dusk, coming home only to bring some groceries to be sold at the shop, and to eat, before going back again to rank in the city. He is a hard worker, that Shadrack. He has no time to rest. That is why he is successful. This is a lesson to you young pipsqueaks who think that things will just fall into your laps like manna from heaven. I told Shadrack about my friend, and after advising me that a car does not move by water but by petrol, I gave him some money to pour petrol into his car. It was fortunate, my brothers and sisters, that I had some money in my shoe where I hide it from my grandchildren. Oops, now they know where I hide my money. But don't worry, I'll find another place. All my pension money went into petrol, my dear brothers and sisters, in order to save the life of my dear friend.

'I am sure that when we took my friend from his house, he was still breathing. But by the time we arrived at the hospital, he was dead. There was nothing that the doctors could do. So we took him to the mortuary instead.'

We are very angry at the needless death of the patriarch, and we condemn his sons for this abomination. Those who come from his ethnic group say that although they don't condone the action of the sons, it was wrong for the deceased to allow the children of the mistress to shave ahead of the proper children. The custom of shaving is crucial, and must be strictly observed. It is almost as important as the custom of filling the grave with soil after the coffin has been lowered into it and all the prayers and orations have been made. The first people to be given the spade to throw soil into the grave are the male relatives. And these must throw the soil in order of their seniority, as with the cutting of hair. Only then can the general public be allowed to fill the grave with soil, and to shape the mound where flowers and wreaths will be laid. Squabbles have often arisen when the names of the male relatives have been called in the incorrect order. But it is unheard of for an elder to be killed by his own children for failing to properly observe the custom. We all agree that the two sons, who are now in prison awaiting trial, deserve to be in jail for the rest of their lives, or to be hanged.

This sad tale confirms what Toloki has long observed. Funerals acquire a life of their own, and give birth to other funerals. The old man's funeral has come about as a direct result of his son's funeral. This was also the case back in the village many years ago, when the choir girl was shot dead at a school-mate's funeral. Indeed, every day we hear of car accidents in which people on their way to or from the funerals of friends or relatives are killed.

After the funeral we solemnly march to the home of the deceased. There we wash our hands in water that has been mixed with the juice of aloes. After this, we wait for the food.

As usual, samp and beef is served in three large basins – almost the size of small bathtubs. One is for the men, the second one for the women, and the third for children. We dip our hands into the samp and, with gravy dripping down our forearms to the elbows, we stuff the food into our mouths.

Toloki is impressed by the care taken with the food. The meat is so soft that even old grandmothers and grandfathers can chew it with their gums. It is well salted, but it is not spiced. Funeral meat is never spiced. It is just boiled in water and seasoned with salt. The samp also is soft and tender. Often the samp at funerals is hard and undercooked.

He looks around, and sees Noria enjoying her food at the basin that is reserved for women. Poor Noria, she only gets to eat meat when there is a funeral. Toloki, on the other hand, does not usually eat at funerals. At first, it was not his choice not to eat. However, when he used to join the men's basin they would make snide remarks about him, and about his odour. Blunt ones would even tell him rudely that he was not welcome at their dish. He could have refused to move, and continued to eat. After all, the food was meant for everyone who was at the funeral, and the louts did not have any special rights over it. But he decided not to lower the dignity of his profession by engaging in quarrels about food. People have been known to fight and injure one another over food at funerals.

At some funerals, especially in the townships where there are better-off people, the system of dispensing food is different. The most important people – usually the relatives and close friends of the family, and those who are pillars of the community – are served food inside the house at the table. The food that is served there will include not only the usual funeral fare of samp and beef, but rice, and some salads, and jelly and custard. The second stratum is made up of those people who are fairly important, but not well-known enough to sit inside at the table. They form a line outside, and women at a table dish samp, beef, and sometimes cabbage onto their individual paper or plastic plates. They eat standing and gossiping about how great and impressive the funeral was, and what inspiring speeches were made, and who has been secretly sleeping with whose wife. The final stratum is that of the rabble. They are fed samp and beef in communal basins, as is done at this funeral in the settlement. The difference in the settlement is that everyone eats like this. The ranked strata do not exist.

At township funerals, Toloki belongs to the second stratum. He usually collects his food, and drifts to some spot where there are no people, and quietly eats from his plate.

No one ever has to stand there and separate people according to their strata. People know who they are and where they belong. These things always work themselves out.

Toloki dips his hand into the samp over and over again. No one complains about him, since the only odour emanating from him is that of perfume. He needs to eat and fill his stomach, especially since he does not know where his next meal will come from. He has some money, but he is far away from the places where he used to buy his luxury food of cakes and green onions. Of course he can buy the normal food of mealie-meal and some relish from a spaza shop, and they can cook it together on the primus stove in the shack. But will Noria agree to that? Won't she say that she doesn't take things from men? He needs to tread lightly, until he has a better understanding of this woman. Or at least until he knows exactly which are the right things to do, and which are the wrong ones.

After the meal, Toloki and Noria go back to their shack. They have some time to kill before she goes to help Madimbhaza, and then to attend her meeting. Toloki has promised to go with her, so as to see what kind of work she does. But first he must change into his civilian clothes. Noria has suggested that he wear his mourning clothes only when he goes to funerals. At home, he must look like other men. It is not a bad idea, really, since it will help to preserve his costume for further years of mourning.

They sit outside the shack and talk about the world, and about death. Noria says she is beginning to get the hang of this mourning business. And she believes that she is able to read meaning into the sounds that he produces. But she needs to attend more funerals with Toloki in order to thoroughly grasp the profound meaning that he draws from the depth of his soul. They try a few sounds together, especially the new goatly sounds. Noria's first attempts are quite amateurish, and they both burst out laughing.

'I am sorry, Toloki, to laugh about such serious matters.'

'Don't be sorry, Noria. In death we laugh as well. Don't you remember that when you were a little girl, your own friend died laughing?'

'You are such a wise man, Toloki.'

Toloki tells her of an occasion, not long ago, when the whole graveyard broke into laughter. There were four funerals taking place at the same time. One of them was a Zionist funeral, and was particularly noisy, since Zionists beat drums and dance around when they pray. At the funeral where he was mourning, things were very solemn, as the family belonged to a denomination that believed in burying their dead with quiet dignity. At the various funerals, preachers were preaching, orators were making their speeches, and people were singing various hymns. Each person was supposed to concentrate on the activities of the funeral she or he was attending, and ignore the noise from other funerals.

The Nurse at the Zionist funeral had a booming voice. Soon, all ears at all four funerals were directed towards him, and people were no longer paying attention to their own funerals. He made a naughty joke about the deceased, and everyone at the various funerals in the cemetery burst out laughing. This happened at the same moment that the priest at the funeral where Toloki was mourning was engaged in the most serious part of the ritual, that of praying for the soul of the deceased so that it should be happily received into the portals of heaven by none other than St Peter himself. Even the priest couldn't help laughing. Everybody laughed for a long time, for it was the kind of joke that seemed to grow on you. You would laugh and eventually stop. But after a few minutes you would think of the joke again, and you would burst out laughing all over again. Laughter kept coming in spurts, with some people even rolling on the ground. When the four processions finally marched off in various directions, some people were still laughing. Others had stomach cramps from laughing too much.

'In our language there is a proverb which says the greatest death is laughter.'

'You see! I was right, Toloki, when I said that you knew how to live.'

Church ministers have spoken at length about heaven, and the infinite joy experienced by those who are lucky enough to go there. Toloki wonders if their joy is as great as the joy he is feeling now, sitting in front of their shack with Noria. The pleasant smell of cheap perfume envelopes them both. It is Toloki's perfume, which he shared with her this morning.

Their conversation drifts to the village. They remember their childhood and their youth. Some memories are happy. Others are sad. But there is no bitterness in either of them. Sometimes they do not see things in the same way. For instance, at one stage Noria says that Jwara was a great man, a great creator who was misunderstood. Toloki chooses not to comment on this. His views on the matter are very different, but why spoil the moment by bringing up contrary opinions about a past that is dead and buried forever?

'I am sorry that I did not go to his funeral, at least to sing for him for the last time. Even now I feel that I still owe him one last song. Things will never be right for me until I have sung that song. One day, when I go back home I will visit his grave, and sing him his last song. Did you mourn at his funeral?'

'No. I learnt of his death long after he had finished dying.'

'I hear his dying was a long process.'

'I heard from Nefolovhodwe that it took many years.'

'The same Nefolovhodwe who pretended that he did not know you and your family? How did he come to discuss Jwara's death with you?'

Toloki tells her that after he became an established Professional Mourner, he remembered his debt to Nefolovhodwe. The woman who was referred to as his wife had given him food. He had vowed that he was going to pay for it once he had the money, as he was not a beggar. He had told both Nefolovhodwe and the woman that he was going to pay back every cent's worth of food that he ate at their house.

* * *

Toloki stood at Nefolovhodwe's gate and rang the bell, summoning the security men to open for him. A guard came and demanded to know what he wanted. He told him that he had come to pay Nefolovhodwe his money. The guard phoned the great man and told him that there was a strange man called Toloki who wanted to pay him his money. He was led into the house.

He was introduced to a petite girl who was referred to as the great man's wife. This one looked young enough to be his granddaughter. Toloki wondered what had happened to the leupa lizard, who had had a heart of gold under her painted exterior.

Nefolovhodwe was sitting at his usual desk, playing with his fleas. The room was different though. The walls were made of marble, and there were small onyx tombstones all around the room. The doors of the room were in the shape of gates made from giant pearls. They were obviously imitation pearls, since no oyster of such size could ever exist.

'Welcome to the Pearly Gates, young man. I thought I was never going to see you again. What do you want this time? A job again?'

Toloki was surprised that the great man remembered him, since on the previous occasion he had proved to have such a short memory. He told him that he did not want a job. He had come to pay for all the food he had eaten in his house. At first Nefolovhodwe felt insulted, but then decided that Toloki must be mad. Perhaps poverty had gone to his head and loosened a few screws.

'Why are you dressed like that?'

'I am a Mourner.'

'Are you mourning for your father?'

'Is he dead?'

'You mean you don't even know that your father is dead?'

Then Nefolovhodwe told him of Jwara's long process of dying. Toloki told him that he was not mourning for Jwara, as he did not even know that he was dead. He was a Professional Mourner who mourned for the nation, and was paid in return. Nefolovhodwe laughed. Toloki walked to his desk and dumped some bank notes on it. He had already determined how much the food he had eaten in that house had cost. Then he walked out with all the dignity he could muster.

'Hey, you come back here, you ugly boy! Don't you see that you have scared my fleas?'

But Toloki did not turn back. He proudly walked straight ahead, until he had left the premises of the man for whom he had lost all respect.

* * *

In the afternoon, Noria and Toloki go to Madimbhaza's house. She says she wants to introduce him to this woman because she is the most important person in her life.

She is an old woman, this Madimbhaza. She lives in a two-roomed shack which is bigger than the usual settlement shack. Many children are playing in the mud outside. Some of the children are on crutches, and some have their legs in callipers. Her home is known by everyone as 'the dumping ground', since women who have unwanted babies dump them in front of her door at night. She feeds and clothes the children out of her measly monthly pension.

Madimbhaza used to work as a domestic servant in the city. She stopped working three months ago when her legs gave in as a result of arthritis. While she was working, Noria and one or two other women from the settlement used to look after the children. They were not paid any salary for this, since Madimbhaza could not have afforded it. Now that she is at home most of the time, the women, Noria in particular, still come every day to help her with the children. They bathe them, and help them dress. Then they feed them, and take those who have reached school-going age to the school that is made out of shipping containers.

'So this is your young man that I hear people talking about so much, Noria.'

'He is not my young man, Madimbhaza. He is my homeboy.'

Toloki shakes her hand. In his mind he sees the little Noria in a gymdress squeaking, 'He's not my brother!' Madimbhaza says she is very happy to meet him, as she has heard so much about him.

Toloki learns that for the past fifteen years Madimbhaza has been taking care of abandoned children. She has often tried to find their biological parents, but usually without success. She says that some mothers have returned to collect their children because of pressure from God, but others have just forgotten about their babies. Some of the children were abandoned because they were born physically handicapped. Others were crippled by polio or other diseases at a later age, and their parents, unable to cope, also abandoned them at the dumping ground. The twilight mum, as Madimbhaza is called in the settlement and the nearby townships, is very proud of all her children.

'God has given me healthy and good children to mother. He knows that I am not young anymore, and that he must give me good children. They all help me around the house and even wash themselves before going to bed at night.'

The twilight mum says that in addition to good children, God has given her good neighbours. Noria is one of the very best.

'That is why, young man, I don't ever want to hear her complain about you. Anyone who hurts Noria hurts me.'

Toloki laughs and promises that Noria will never have cause to complain about him.

Some of the children are victims of the war that is raging in the land. Their parents died in massacres and in train slaughters. In a recent massacre in the settlement, which was carried out by some of the tribal chief's followers from the hostels, assisted by Battalion 77 of the armed forces of the government, as many as fifty-two people died, including children. Some children were orphaned overnight. They are now here at the dumping ground.

'All I want to do in life now is to give them a good start and teach them to be good human beings when they grow up. I will die a very happy person if this can be done. These children are all very special to me. I treat them as my very own and they regard me as their mother. Nothing can ever take them away from me.'

Toloki wonders how this brave and kind woman has survived all these years, with so many mouths to feed. Noria tells him that through all the years she made do with her own meagre earnings. Our elders say that an elephant does not find its own trunk heavy. It was only last month that Madimbhaza received assistance for the first time. A newspaper, *City Press*, wrote a story about her. As a result, some kind readers donated clothes and blankets for the children.

It dawns on Toloki for the first time that Noria is still very young at thirty-five. She is handicapped neither physically nor mentally. She is strong, and does not drink. She does not abuse drugs in any form whatsoever. Surely she could have taken a job as a domestic worker. Or as an office cleaner – a job she has some experience in, having done it in the small town back home. She could even sell fat cakes and fruit on the streets. But she has chosen to spend her days working at the dumping ground.

It is Noria who knows how to live.

9

Women are singing, while they slice loaves of bread on a long makeshift table. Others cut cabbage. Their song is about the freedom that is surely coming tomorrow. They also sing about the enemy that will be defeated, and about the tribal chief who will die like a dog one day. Sometimes they sing about sad things that have happened to their people. Yet their jubilation belies the sadness of their message. It is like those political funerals where the Young Tigers dance to a call-and-response chant. Someone who does not understand the meaning in these chants might be amazed or even shocked at how these youths can be so happy at a funeral. Perhaps the jubilation is due to the fact that part of the message of the songs is that the people shall be victorious in the end.

The women are excited when Noria arrives with Toloki.

'Hey Noria, you have come with your mate.'

'Yes, so that he should see the work that we do.'

'That is very good, Noria. Our men must see what we are doing, so that when we come home late they cannot complain.'

'He is not my man. He is my homeboy.'

The women laugh, and say that it is good that homeboys these days move in with their homegirls. They go on teasing about how people from the same village must look after one another, and satisfy each other's needs. Noria ignores the remarks, and joins the women in cutting the cabbage. She already knows how naughty her friends can be. Toloki, on the other hand, is embarrassed. He is the only man among all these chattering females.

He recognises the stout 'Malehlohonolo, and shyly smiles at her. She returns the smile.

'Hello, I saw you this morning when you were washing yourself.'

'Yes, I remember you. I heard Noria say that you were going to do washing in the city.'

'Some of us have to work. We don't all live on the Holy Spirit like your woman.'

'She is not my woman. She is my homegirl.'

The women burst out laughing again. Toloki wonders what is funny about being Noria's homeboy.

He learns that the women are preparing food for a community meeting that will take place later that afternoon. Some of the leaders of the political movement will be coming to discuss the problems of the residents. One major problem is that of security. From time to time, the settlement has been invaded by the migrants from the hostels, and by soldiers from Battalion 77, who are specially recruited and trained in dirty tricks. This battalion, which includes foreign mercenaries from a destabilised neighbouring country, is particularly vicious, and slaughters mercilessly because it is composed of foreign mercenaries.

The women prepare to put the cabbage in a big three-legged pot. Noria asks Toloki to help with the water. He is shown three plastic containers and a wheelbarrow. He pushes the whole load to a communal tap a few streets away. He stands patiently in a long queue of children and women who have also come to draw water. When his turn comes, he fills the containers with water, loads them on the wheelbarrow, and pushes it back to the school. Although he is still embarrassed at being the only man working with women, he feels happy knowing that he has been of assistance to Noria. He is doing all this for Noria, and not for anyone else, nor for anything else.

Noria pours the water into the pot, under which a wood fire is already burning. Then she puts the finely cut cabbage, together with a lot of beef stock and curry powder, into the pot.

She uses very little salt, since beef stock already has salt in it. As the cabbage boils, some young men and women bring chairs and a small table from different neighbouring shacks. All the time they continue to sing songs of freedom, as they arrange the chairs for the meeting. More people gather. Most of them are women, but there are also a few men. Toloki feels more comfortable when the men arrive.

After an hour or so, a big black Mercedes Benz followed by several other smaller cars drives into the school yard. Women ululate and men shout slogans. The Young Tigers form a guard of honour, as the leaders walk from their cars, and are seated on the chairs. Noria whispers to Toloki that the man who arrived in the big black car and his wife are both members of the national executive of the political movement. The others are various branch and local committee members.

The meeting begins. The leaders listen to the grievances of the people, and long debates ensue. There is a squabble among some members of the street committee, and the leaders are asked to solve it. Not knowing the internal politics of the settlement, Toloki cannot make sense of what the argument is about. It sounds quite petty to him – something about committee members who have usurped the powers of others, and about misuse of funds. Toloki notices that the people who are most active in the affairs of the settlement are the women. Not only do they do all the work, but they play leadership roles. At this meeting, they present the most practical ideas to solve the various problems. The few male residents who are present relish making high-flown speeches that display eloquence, but are short on practical solutions.

After the street committee squabble has been solved the next item on the agenda is the preparations for a big demonstration that will take place in the city next week. There is going to be a stayaway from work for the whole of that week. The people are beginning the new year with a strong statement to the government that it is high time that they took the negotiations for freedom seriously. The position of the people is stated clearly by 'Malehlohonolo when she addresses the meeting.

'While our leaders are talking with the government to put things right, the government is busy killing us with its Battalion 77, and its vigilantes. What kind of negotiations are these where on one hand they talk of peace and freedom, and on the other, they kill us dead?'

After each speech, the Young Tigers lead the people in song and dance. They chant praises of the political leaders who have suffered years of imprisonment and exile, fighting for the freedom of their people. They also chant strong condemnation of those they refer to as sell-outs.

'Death to the sell-outs! Down with the sell-outs!'

Other speakers address the problem of the tribal chief and his followers from the hostels. They say that the tribal chief has delusions that he can destroy the common goal of the people. But the people are united, and shall fight to the bitter end for their liberation.

After these stirring speeches, a committee of five is elected to organise the stayaway in the settlement. Noria is one of those who are elected. They will go from house to house, explaining to people why they should not go to work.

After the meeting, food is served on paper plates. The leaders are served on enamel plates. During the meal, they call Noria to join them at their table, as they want to speak with her privately. Noria, however, is in awe of these great people, and does not sit down. She stands respectfully in front of the high-powered couple. They express their heartfelt sorrow at the death of her son. They say it was a regrettable mistake. But they warn Noria very strongly that she must not speak to anyone about it, especially the newspaper people, because this would take the struggle for freedom a step backwards. She

173

must remember that her son was not completely innocent in this whole matter.

'We are very happy that you have been elected onto the stay-away committee. This shows that we, as a movement, have nothing against you personally. We love you as one of our own. Whoever burnt down your shack did a very cruel thing. We don't agree with it at all. We absolutely condemn it, in fact.'

The bejewelled woman smiles benevolently at her. Noria listens silently, and then walks away without saying a word. She feels that there is nothing she can say, because the leaders are talking at her, and are not actually discussing the death of her son with her at all. Their apology is made privately, and not at the public meeting, as the local street committee had promised, and is accompanied by a rider about her son's guilt. This fills her with anger.

Everyone is happy that the meeting has been such a great success. Everyone except Noria, who feels betrayed. However, she joins in the song and dance that follows the meal, and no one knows of the heavy sadness that occupies her heart.

The leaders drive away, and the men remain behind to blame the women for disgracing the whole settlement community in front of the honourable leadership of the movement. As the women clear the tables, the men reprove them in utter disgust.

'How can you serve bread and cabbage to our important leaders?'

'What did you want us to serve them?'

'Proper food that befits our leaders. Were you too lazy to cook meat, and potatoes, and rice, and to make salads?'

'We are poor people. We can only give them what we ourselves eat. They must see our poverty. We cannot pretend to them that we are meat and rice people, when in fact our daily supper is pap and water. As a matter of fact, we gave them a treat. We don't normally eat bread.'

'You talk just like women. Our disgrace will be told in all the communities around the country. We will never live down this shame.'

'Perhaps if you were here, you could have given us money, and also helped us cook your meat and potatoes.'

As Toloki and Noria walk back to their home, they call at each shack along the way, and Noria tells those who live there about the stayaway. Most people agree that it is a necessary step, and say that they will observe it. Some shacks are empty because the owners are still singing and dancing in the school yard. One or two others ask her if the movement will feed their children when they lose their jobs. Noria patiently explains that if people all act together, they will not lose their jobs. The employers cannot sack every worker in the land.

Toloki notices that in every shack they visit, the women are never still. They are always doing something with their hands. They are cooking. They are sewing. They are outside scolding the children. They are at the tap drawing water. They are washing clothes. They are sweeping the floor in their shacks, and the ground outside. They are closing holes in the shacks with cardboard and plastic. They are loudly joking with their neighbours while they hang washing on the line. Or they are fighting with the neighbours about children who have beaten up their own children. They are preparing to go to the taxi rank to catch taxis to the city, where they will work in the kitchens of their madams. They are always on the move. They are always on the go.

Men, on the other hand, tend to cloud their heads with pettiness and vain pride. They sit all day and dispense wide-ranging philosophies on how things should be. With great authority in their voices, they come up with wise theories on how to put the world right. Then at night they demand to be given food, as if the food just walked into the house on its own. When they believe all the children are asleep, they want to be

175

pleasured. The next day they wake up and continue with their empty theories.

Toloki hesitantly mentions these observations to Noria. He attributes his keen sense of observation to the fact that he has not lived with other human beings for many years. He therefore sees things with a fresh eye. Some of the things he sees are things he would otherwise have taken for granted, if he had been part of the community in which they happened. Like other men he would assume that it was normal for things to be like this, for surely this is how they were meant to be from day one of creation. Noria listens to these ideas with astonishment.

Toloki wonders further why it is that the people who do all the work at the settlement are women, yet all the national and regional leaders he saw at the meeting were men – except, of course, for the bejewelled wife of the Mercedes Benz leader, who is also an elected leader in her own right.

'You are right, Toloki. And I hear that it is not only here where the situation is as you describe. All over the country, in what the politicians call grassroot communities, women take the lead. But very few women ever reach the executive level. Or even the regional or branch committee levels. I don't know why it is like this, Toloki.'

'You know what I think, Noria? From what I have seen today, I believe the salvation of the settlement lies in the hands of women.'

'You amaze me every day, Toloki. You come with things I don't expect. Yes, when we were growing up, women had no names. They were called Mother of Toloki or Mother of Noria. But here women are leaders of the people.'

Again they find themselves holding hands as they walk towards their shack. But now they are not embarrassed, and they do not pull away. They make a strikingly lovely picture against the sunset: she of the poppy-seed beauty, and he of the complexion that is yellow like the ochre of the village. She of the willowy stature in a red and white polka-dot dress, he of the squat and stocky body in khaki pants and shirt. Their grotesquely tall shadows accentuate the disparity in their heights. They trudge the ground with their cracked feet in the same tired rhythm. Toloki decided that since Noria had no shoes, he was not going to wear any shoes either.

They walk into the shack.

'Did you have enough to eat at the meeting?'

'I am fine, Noria. The way you women cooked that cabbage, it tasted just like meat.'

'Perhaps we should take a walk in the garden before we sleep. It is beautiful to walk among the flowers with you, Toloki.'

'Yes, let us walk in the garden.'

However, they do not walk in the garden. They stare at the pictures on the wall, but are unable to evoke the enchantment. They concentrate very hard, without success. Noria bursts out crying, and apologises to Toloki. She says it is all her fault. Her mind is full of too many things that are not pleasant. Toloki is certain that these are the first real tears he has seen from Noria. At the funeral on Christmas Day she did break down into sobs, but he did not see her tears. There were too many people around her. But now, with his own hands, he is wiping her tears away. He is overwhelmed by sadness, and his own eyes fill with tears as well.

'Don't worry, Noria. We'll surely walk in the garden tomorrow.'

'It is not that, Toloki. I know that as long as you are here, you will transport us to the garden, and we shall be happy again. It is just that I feel so betrayed!'

She tells him that the local street committee had promised her that the leaders would publicly make a statement at the meeting, apologising for the death of her son, and reprimanding those who were responsible for it. Instead, they called her privately, and added insult to injury by saying that her child, who was only five years old, was not completely blameless.

'Who killed your son, Noria?'

'The Young Tigers.'

'And they burnt down your shack?'

'No one knows who burnt my shack down. It must be the same people who killed my son. Maybe to intimidate me ... to keep me quiet ... or to silence me forever.'

'Keep you quiet? Is it a secret then, that the Young Tigers are responsible? Don't the people know?'

Noria explains that the people know very well. The whole country knows. At least, those people who read newspapers since the story was featured prominently, with all the gory pictures. The kind of silence that everyone is demanding from her is that she should not condemn the perpetrators in any public forum, as this would give ammunition to the enemy. Now she sees that what they really want is that she, like the rest of the community, should accept her child's guilt, and take it that he received what he deserved. If she keeps quiet, the whole scandal will quietly die, and no one will point fingers and say, 'You see, they say they are fighting for freedom, yet they are no different from the tribal chief and his followers. They commit atrocities as well.'

Noria, however, refuses to be silenced, and tells Toloki that she will fight to the end to see that justice is done. She has kept quiet all these days because she believed that when the national leaders came, they would address the matter openly and with fairness, instead of sweeping it under the carpet.

'They have treated you like this, yet you continue to work for them.'

'I am not working for them, but for my people.'

'I don't read newspapers, so I do not know how your son died. But I am prepared to fight with you, Noria.'

* * *

Vutha's second death. It all started with the last massacre experienced by the residents of the settlement. Perhaps we should say that it actually began with his involvement in what we call the struggle. At the age of five, Vutha was already a veteran of many political demonstrations. He was an expert at dancing the freedom dance, and at chanting the names of the leaders who must be revered, and of the sell-outs who must be destroyed. He could recite the Liberation Code and the Declaration of the People's Rights. Of course, he did not understand a single word, since it was all in English. He mispronounced most of the words, too. He also knew all the songs. Even when he was playing with mud in the streets, or with wire cars with the other children, he could be heard singing about freedom, and about the heroic deeds of the armed wing of the people's movement. He, of course, was not displaying any particular precociousness in this regard. All the children of the settlement, even those younger than Vutha, were (and still are) well-versed in these matters.

Noria was very proud of her son's political involvement. She also was very active in demonstrations. She and her friend, 'Malehlohonolo, never missed a single demonstration. Even though 'Malehlohonolo was a washerwoman in the city, she would arrange her schedule around demonstrations and other political activities in the settlement. For her, the struggle came first.

When 'Malehlohonolo went to work in the city, she left her four-year-old daughter, Danisa, with Noria. Danisa played together with Vutha in the mud. They built mud houses, in which they baked mud pies.

They sang freedom songs, and danced the freedom dance. Sometimes Vutha, who was a year older than Danisa, would bully and slap her. She would cry and go to report to Auntie Noria. Auntie Noria would be angry with Vutha, and she would spank him.

'Vutha, you don't know how to play with other children. I'll beat you until your buttocks are sour.'

After the spanking, Vutha would run away crying. He would then throw stones at the shack, while singing a freedom song with the message that his mother was a sell-out who should be destroyed along with the tribal chief. Noria would then chase after him. He knew from experience that he could not outrun his mother. She would catch him and spank him again. At first he would fight back, and bite his mother, while yelling for the whole world to hear that his mother was killing him. But when Noria did not stop, he would beg for forgiveness, and promise that he would never do it again, that he would be a good boy. Danisa would also be screaming at the same time, 'Auntie Noria! Please forgive The Second, I know he won't beat me up again'. She would try to bite Noria's hand in order to save Vutha.

'The Second is my brother! Please don't kill him, Auntie Noria!'

After a few minutes they would all forget about the incident, and would be happily singing again. Noria would give them the sugared soft porridge that 'Malehlohonolo left for them in the morning when she went to work.

Although Noria was proud that her son was a political activist, she worried whenever there were demonstrations. Vutha was always in the forefront of the stone throwers. Soldiers and police sometimes came in armoured vehicles to confront the demonstrators. Vutha and his comrades would throw stones at the armoured vehicles. The soldiers, challenged by the full might of deadly five-year-olds armed with arsenals of stones, would open fire. In many cases, children died in these clashes. Noria always warned her son about fighting wars with the soldiers. It was one thing to demonstrate and sing freedom songs and dance the freedom dance. But to face soldiers who were armed with machine guns was much too dangerous. She didn't want to lose her son for the second time, and she told him so.

'But mama, I am a cadre. I am a freedom fighter.'

'It is a good thing to be a cadre, my child. But when the soldiers come, you must not be in the front. Let the older boys, the Young Tigers, be in the frontline.'

'I am not a coward, mama. I am a Young Tiger too.'

The Young Tigers form the youth wing of the political movement. The core group is usually made up of youths, both male and female, in their late teens and early twenties. However, there are some peripheral members who are much older, sometimes even in their thirties. Younger activists of Vutha's age generally regard themselves as Young Tigers too.

The Young Tigers always praised Vutha for the strength of his throw. They said that if a stone from his hand hit a policeman, or a soldier, or a hostel vigilante on the head, he would surely fall down. Vutha was proud of this praise that came from older and battle-scarred cadres. It established him as a hero among his peers. Sometimes it went to his head, hence his practising his stone-throwing skills at Noria's shack whenever she punished him for being a bad boy.

Often the Young Tigers gave the children political education. They taught them about the nature of oppression, the history of the movement, why it became necessary to wage an armed struggle, why it was recently suspended, why the tribal chief was doing such dirty things to the people, and how the government had been forced to unban the political movement of the people and to negotiate with its leaders. Much of this information floated above the heads of the children. This did not bother the Young Tigers. They knew that whatever little information the children grasped, it would make them committed freedom fighters, and upright leaders of tomorrow.

One night, when the settlement was deep in sleep, Battalion 77, supported by migrants from a nearby hostel, invaded. They attacked at random, burning the shacks. When the residents ran out, sometimes naked, the hostel inmates, uttering their famous war-cry, chopped them down with their pangas and stabbed them with their spears. The soldiers of Battalion 77 opened fire. They entered some shacks, and raped the women. They cut the men down after forcing them to watch their wives and daughters being raped. In one shack, a woman who was nine months pregnant was stabbed with a spear. As she lay there dying, she went into labour. Only the head of the baby had appeared, when it was hacked off with a panga by yet another warrior.

The whole exercise took less than thirty minutes, and in no time the invaders had disappeared into thin air. Those who had survived went to report to the police, who only came to investigate three hours after the bloody event.

The next morning, the entire settlement was dotted with smouldering ruins. Fifty-two people were dead, and more than a hundred others were in hospital with serious injuries.

Statements of accusation and denial were flying through the air. The residents and the political movement were pointing a finger at the hostel migrants and Battalion 77. The government was denying that Battalion 77 was involved, and the tribal chief was denying that his followers had anything to do with it. It was a terrible thing that had happened, he said, but anyone who wanted to blame his followers had to come up with evidence. It was not enough to say that someone saw the invaders coming from the direction of the hostels, and that they spoke the language of the tribal chief's ethnic group. People had the right to speak any language they liked, and this could not, by any stretch of imagination, make them killers. Moreover, the tribal chief added, the residents of the settlement liked to attack the hostel inmates whenever they got the opportunity. Many of his followers had been killed and no one was saying a word about it.

Noria was fortunate in that her shack was untouched. So was 'Malehlohonolo's. They went to help the unluckier families. In many cases, there was nothing they could do. The whole family had been wiped out. In other cases, there were survivors. They took new orphans to the dumping ground, where they were welcomed with open arms by Madimbhaza.

For many days that followed, a dark cloud hovered over the settlement. There was anger mingled with bitterness. People had lost friends and relatives. Husbands had lost wives, and wives had lost husbands. Children had lost parents, and siblings.

The funeral was the biggest that had ever been seen in those parts. The president of the political movement was there in person, together with the rest of his national executive. He, the consummate statesman as always, made a conciliatory speech, in which he called upon the people to lay down their arms and work towards building a new future of peace and freedom. He called those who had died martyrs whose blood would, in the standard metaphor for all those who had fallen in the liberation struggle, water the tree of freedom. He called upon the government to stop its double agenda of negotiating for a new order with the leaders of the political movement, while destabilizing the communities by killing their residents, and by assassinating political leaders. He further called upon the tribal chief to stop his gory activities, and to walk the democratic path.

The national president of the Young Tigers, however, was on the war-path. In his fiery speech he called upon his followers to avenge the deaths of their fathers, mothers, brothers and sisters.

'We cannot just sit and fold our arms while they continue to kill us. The people must now defend themselves. Those who were in the armed wing of the political movement, who came back home when amnesty was declared and the armed struggle was suspended, must help our communities to form defence units. Our people shall not die in vain. Every death shall be avenged!'

After the prayers and the speeches, fifty-two coffins of varying size were lowered into the fifty-two graves. Fifty-two mounds of fresh soil were shaped with shovels and spades, and wreaths were laid. Some of the messages that were read came from presidents and prime ministers from all over the world. Ambassadors representing foreign countries were among the dignitaries who were at the funeral. There was no one who was not disgusted with the senseless killing. Indeed, the residents of the settlement saw that they were not alone in their hour of bereavement.

After the funeral, the task of rebuilding began in earnest. The people were determined to show the tribal chief, and the dirty tricks department of the government, that they would not be destroyed. Their will to survive, and to live to see the freedom that was surely coming soon, was too strong to be destroyed by any massacre.

There was a flurry of activity in the settlement. Street committees met, and planned strategies on how to defend the community. The Young Tigers formed neighbourhood patrols, and interrogated every stranger they saw loitering around the settlement. They stopped cars and demanded identification from the drivers and the passengers. A few stubborn drivers who did not want to co-operate were beaten up. Sometimes their money and watches were confiscated as well, although the leaders of the Young Tigers strenuously denied that they were responsible for such actions. They said it was not the policy of the organization to rob innocent motorists. The agents of the state were responsible for these nefarious activities, in order to sully the name of the Young Tigers.

Each afternoon, the local leadership of the Young Tigers called a meeting in which strategies were discussed. Vutha, Danisa, and other children of their age who had already established their reputations as political activists, always attended these meetings. They might not have understood everything that was happening there, but everyone took their presence quite seriously, as they were the leaders of tomorrow.

After school, the children of the settlement used to play in the marshlands that divided the settlement and a township where some of the hostels were located. In fact, the hostels were on the edge of the township, and faced directly over the marshlands. Vutha, and some of the children of his age who were waiting to be seven so that they could go to school, sometimes played there during school hours. They improvised fishing lines and caught frogs and old shoes in the mosquito-infested ponds.

Noria did not like the children to play in the marshlands because she said it was too dangerous. When it had rained heavily in the past, children had drowned in those marshlands, since the ponds turned into small lakes. She preferred to keep an eye on Vutha and Danisa at all times. They accompanied her to the dumping ground whenever she felt Madimbhaza needed her help. When she drew water for the shebeen queens the children tagged along to the communal tap, and to the shebeens as well.

One day a shebeen queen came to ask Noria to draw water for her. She needed many buckets of water because she was going to brew a lot of beer for the weekend. Noria called Vutha to follow her to the tap. Danisa was at home, since 'Malehlohonolo had not gone to do washing that day. She walked a few steps and turned, only to find that Vutha was not there. He had remained behind.

'Hey wena Vutha! Didn't I say you must follow me?'

'I am coming, mama. I'll find you at the tap.'

But Vutha didn't come. Instead he went to the marshlands to catch frogs and punish them for being frogs by punching holes in their bodies with a safety pin. There he found a friend from the neighbourhood, an eight-year-old boy who did not like going to school. He had left home pretending he was going to school, but had gone to fish in the marshlands instead.

While they were playing together, three men approached them. They tried to run away, but the men were too fast. They caught them, and asked them who they were. They wanted to know the names of their parents, and where they lived. The children knew immediately that these men were hostel dwellers. They screamed and begged for mercy.

'Don't cry, my children. We are not going to do anything to you. Come with us.'

They dragged them screaming and kicking their legs across the marshlands to the hostels. Here they took them into one of the hostel dormitories, where there were men sitting on cement beds. Some were joking and laughing, while others were playing their guitars, singing of faraway valleys and beautiful maidens, and cattle that were dying because of drought. Others were cooking on primus stoves, and the smell of meat filled the room. The men took the children to their own corner of the dormitory. There they fed them quantities of meat and steamed bread. They gave them the fermented maize drink known as mageu to wash down the food. The children had never feasted so much in their lives. After a banquet fit for a king, the men told them to go home.

'You see, we are not as bad as you squatters make us out to be. You can come for more meat tomorrow. You'll find us here. But don't tell your parents about this. They won't allow you to come if they know.'

The children went back to the settlement with their secret. The older boy did not trust Vutha. He thought that he would burst out and boast to his friends about his illicit adventure. The friends would in turn tell their parents, and that would be the end of their feasting on meat.

'Hey wena The Second, if ever you tell anyone about this, I will beat you up, and cut off your ears, and feed them to my dog.'

When Vutha got home, Noria was very angry. She demanded to know where he had gone when he had promised to follow her to the tap.

'I went to play in the marshlands, mama.'

Noria threatened to give him a thorough hiding. He cried and asked for mercy. Noria decided not to punish him. At least he had not gone there with Danisa. She did not want to answer to 'Malehlohonolo if the children drowned, or if anything terrible happened to them. Things of that nature spoilt friendships.

That afternoon, Vutha went to the usual political meetings. His marshlands friend was there. So was Danisa. After the lessons, the children participated in the usual democratic forum where the older Young Tigers discussed strategies for self-defence. There was going to be a rally of the followers of the tribal chief at the big central stadium the following Saturday afternoon. Buses were going to transport his followers there from all over the country, since it was essential that the rally should be a very big one. This would show the hostile media that the tribal chief had a lot of support. The Young Tigers' plan was to ambush one of the buses from the hostel at a particular spot on its way to the rally, and to mow down all the passengers with semi-automatic rifles. This would be a fitting vengeance for the massacre.

The next day 'Malehlohonolo brought Danisa to Noria's shack, and left for the city. Noria carried on with her chores while the children played their usual games. They tagged along when she went to the dumping ground, and to draw water for the brewers. But after some time Noria noticed that only Danisa was tagging along. Vutha was not there.

'What happened to Vutha, Danisa?'

'A big boy came and took him away. I think they went to the marshlands.'

'Why didn't you tell me, Danisa?'

'The Second said he was going to beat me up if I told.'

Vutha and his friend had meanwhile gone to their hostel friends, who gave them plenty of meat and pap. They also stuffed their pockets with sweets. Then they asked them about the meetings. They wanted to know what the Young Tigers were planning. At first the children were reluctant to talk. But the men assured them that no one would ever know that they had divulged any information to them.

'And we are going to give you some more meat, and sweets too.'

The older boy started blurting out the information about the planned ambush. He was vague about the details, since strategies of warfare are not easy for children to grasp. However, the information was enough to give the hostel dwellers an indication that something was being planned by the Young Tigers, and roughly what form it would take. They sent the children home with promises of more sweets and meat if they continued to visit them, and brought them any more information that they might have at their disposal.

Unfortunately when they left the hostel, school was out, and a lot of the settlement children were already playing in the marshlands. They were seen and questioned about what they were doing at the hostel. At first, they denied that they were ever there, but the older boys pressed them, and said that they were going to tell when they got back home. Vutha and his friend shared their sweets with them, in a futile attempt to buy their silence. When these children got home, they told their parents that Vutha and his friend had been at the hostel, and were given sweets by the hostel inmates. Some of the older residents said that maybe the hostel dwellers were trying to sue for peace with the settlement by bribing their children with sweets.

The Young Tigers, however, took a different view. They questioned the children sternly about their activities at the hostel.

'The hostel dwellers are not your uncles. They cannot just give you sweets for nothing. What did you promise them? What did you tell them?'

The children had to confess that they told the hostel inmates about the planned ambush. The leaders of the Young Tigers were very angry. They called all the children to come and see what happened to sell-outs. They put a tyre around Vutha's small neck, and around his friend's. They filled both tyres with petrol. Then they gave boxes of matches to Danisa and to a boy of roughly the same age.

'Please forgive us! We'll never do it again. We are very sorry for what we did.'

'Oh, mother! Where is my mother!'

'Shut up, you sell-outs! Now, all of you children who have gathered here, watch and see what happens to sell-outs. Know that if you ever become a sell-out, this is what will happen to you as well. Now you two, light the matches, and throw them at the tyres.'

Danisa and the child who had been given the honour of carrying out the execution struck their matches, and threw them at the tyres. Danisa's match fell into Vutha's tyre. It suddenly burst into flames. His screams were swallowed by the raging flames, the crackle of burning flesh, and the blowing wind. He tried to run, but the weight of the tyre pulled him to the ground, and he fell down. The eight-year-old was able to stagger for some distance, but he also fell down in a ball of fire that rolled for a while and then stopped. Soon the air was filled with the stench of burning flesh. The children watched for a while, then ran away to their mothers.

Danisa also ran to her home. 'Malehlohonolo was not back from the city yet. So she ran to Noria's.

'Auntie Noria, I burnt The Second because he is a sell-out.'

Noria could not understand what the excited little girl was talking about. But she followed Danisa, who promised that she would lead her to where she had burnt the boy. By the time they arrived there, many people had already gathered. They had also heard from their children how sell-outs were set on fire on the instructions of the Young Tigers. The tyres were still smouldering, but the remains of the two boys were charred and shrivelled. Noria threw herself on the ground and wailed.

'Oh, Vutha my child, you can't die again!'

Noria was transformed into a madwoman. Throughout that night, she roamed around the settlement shouting that she wanted the bastards who had killed her son. She was prepared to kill them with her own bare hands, she said.

'Where are you, you cowards? Why don't you come out and face me? I will not rest until I expose you! Until I make you taste the same death!'

Towards dawn, her voice became hoarse. Although she was not yet tired of going from street to street, she could not yell her challenge to the killers anymore. She went back to her shack, only to find it a sheet of flame. She fled to Madimbhaza's dumping ground.

The whole community was numbed by what had happened. Different views were proffered. Some felt that the Young Tigers had gone too far in their protection of the settlement. Others reserved their opinions. But one strange thing was that none of the children could say who was actually responsible for the atrocity. They just said it was the Young Tigers. Who in particular? Just the Young Tigers. Who had given the instructions to Danisa and the other child to light the tyres? The Young Tigers. Who among the Young Tigers? Just the Young Tigers.

* * *

'Do you understand how I feel, Toloki, to be told that my child deserved to die like that, after I carried him in my womb for thirty months?'

'Thirty months, Noria?'

'I am not making a mistake, Toloki. The first time I carried him for fifteen months, which is a long time for any woman to carry a baby. He was born, and Napu fed him to the dogs. I carried him again for another fifteen months. He died for the second time when the Young Tigers set him on fire.'

Toloki wants to know if no one was arrested for this atrocity. Noria says that the police are still investigating. They have had great difficulty in finding witnesses, so they are unable to say who gave the order to have the boys set alight. They cannot arrest Danisa and the other child, since they are babies.

'Up to this day I do not want to see Danisa. Not because I blame her, you understand? But because she reminds me so much of my child. And the poor girl is going to have to live with this for the rest of her life. At first 'Malehlohonolo was afraid to face me. But I assured her that she should not blame herself. If anyone is to blame, it is myself. Both children were under my care when it happened.'

'You are not to blame either, Noria.'

They fall into their by now customary moments of silence, when each one is lost in his or her thoughts. Tears roll down Toloki's cheeks. He is ashamed to be seen crying like this. After all he is a man, is he not? Noria smiles reassuringly at him, and wipes his tears with the back of her hand. She suggests that they both take a bath, as this will make them feel better. Although he does not understand how a bath will make them feel better, he agrees. He is willing to learn new ways of living. After all, Noria herself was quite willing to learn how to walk in the garden with him, to the extent that she is now a garden enthusiast in her own right.

She lights the primus stove and warms some water in a big tin. She pours the water into a washing basin, and mixes it with the juice of aloes. She asks Toloki to take his clothes off. Toloki is taken aback. He thought that each one of them was going to bathe outside the shack in turn, as they had done in the morning. She meanwhile takes off all her clothes, unveiling her womanhood to him. She stands there completely naked, as if lost in a reverie. Toloki follows like a sheep to slaughter. He also takes off his clothes and unveils his maleness. They both kneel over the basin, and with their washing rags, bathe each other with the aloed water. They dazedly rub each other's backs, and slowly move down to other parts of their bodies. It is as though they are responding to rhythms that are silent for the rest of the world, and can only be heard or felt by them. They take turns to stand in the basin, and splash water on each other's bodies. All this they do in absolute silence, and their movements are slow and deliberate. They are in a dream-like state, their thoughts concentrated only on what they are doing to each other. Nothing else matters. Nothing else exists.

After drying each other with their cloths, Noria opens the door and throws the remaining water outside. Most of it has spattered on the floor. Toloki takes his perfume from his trolley, and gives it to her. She splashes some of it on his body. He does likewise to her body.

Without saying a word to each other, they spread their blankets on the floor, and doss down – in their separate kingdoms.

IO

Tuesday morning. New Year's Eve. Noria is still fast asleep, and snoring loudly, when Toloki wakes up. He is no longer afraid to feast his eyes on the contours of her body that delicately map the donkey blanket. It is no longer rape, since last night she allowed him to look, and to touch. Last night was like a vision that confirmed that Noria is indeed a goddess. And he was so proud of himself. His body had not betrayed him by having its blood run amok to parts that were prone to getting throbbingly stiff. Nothing got wet, except from the water that Noria had kept on splashing all over his body. Throughout the night he had slept peacefully, and had not been bothered by crude dreams.

For the first time since leaving the village, he had slept naked. Noria had slept naked too, which was a dangerous thing for both of them to do. Smart settlement people never sleep naked, since they don't know when the next invasion will be. When a massacre takes place one should be able to run away fully clothed. If one has to die, one should at least die with one's clothes on, so that when they come the next day to gawp at the corpses, and to photograph them for posterity, the body parts deserving of respect and privacy are not displayed to the world.

He dresses in his khaki home clothes, and prepares to leave. But before he opens the door, he remembers that Noria insists that he wash himself every day. He gets his washing rag, which is slightly wet from last night, and cleans his face, and his armpits. He sniffs the cloth, and decides that it does not smell. After all, he reasons, he is still clean from last night's bath.

He takes a last look at Noria, who sleeps peacefully in the traditional foetal position. He blows her a kiss, and walks away. He really does not know where he is going. And why he is going. He needs to think. He walks slowly towards the taxi rank. It is teeming with excited people, who are already filled with the New Year spirit. Taxi boys are touting passengers. Some even go to the extent of pulling confused old ladies onto their taxis, without even asking where they are going. He gets into one of the taxis, which quickly fills up and drives away. Passengers are packed like sardines in this old vehicle. He therefore cannot see outside, and does not know where the taxi is going. He does not care.

Passengers are talking about the New Year parties they will be attending. For many, this is the most exciting holiday of the year. Even more exciting than Christmas. The revelling starts on New Year's Eve, with people singing and dancing and getting generally drunk and rowdy. No one sleeps on New Year's Eve, at least not until the bells toll midnight, and a new year is born with its new problems. On the first day of the new year, the young children dress in their new clothes. In many cases, these are the clothes they wore on Christmas Day. Those whose parents can afford it, buy two sets of new clothes, one for Christmas and the second for New Year. But it is rare for parents to be able to afford this. Most children would rather not wear their new clothes on Christmas Day, so that they can save them for New Year's Day.

Those who are teenagers do not wear any new clothes at all on New Year's Day. Instead, they cross-dress. Boys wear dresses, and stuff pillows into their pants and rags into their shirts to make exaggerated buttocks and breasts. They paint their faces with plenty of blusher, and smear thick layers of lip-stick on their lips, and darken their eyelashes with mascara. Girls wear old trousers, shirts, jackets and ties borrowed from their fathers. They smear their faces with black shoe polish. After this elaborate make-up, the teens go from house to house shouting 'Happe-eee!', the same way that younger children do on Christmas Day when they enter each house asking for a 'Christmas box.' When the cross-dressed teens enter each house, they ask for a 'Happy New Year.' This means that they are asking for delicacies such as cakes, ginger beer, and sweets, which very few families do not provide on days like these.

A lot of the passengers are going to do last minute-shopping in the city, especially for wine and brandy. Some are just going to watch the parades, and while away time until the evening revels begin back in the settlements or in the townships. A few others are going to ply their pickpocketing trade, and to carry out the various con tricks from which they earn their living.

The taxi stops in the central business district. He alights and walks in the familiar streets. They are decorated with lights of different colours, and with banners and bunting – all in preparation for the parades that will take place in the afternoon to celebrate the New Year. Over the years, Toloki has watched many of these parades of colourful dancers with painted faces, dressed in silk suits. Their clownish antics and their funny songs always make the spectators on the pavements laugh. There are always marching bands and drum majorettes. He has marched with the bands every year – they on the cleared streets, he on the sidewalks. The traffic police are already clearing the streets for the carnival. This day is one of the highlights of the year, when we are all carefree and forget about the problems that live with us the whole year round.

He wanders aimlessly, until he finds himself at the waterfront among the tourists. Since he is not wearing his professional costume, they don't pay any particular attention to him, except of course to make sure that their wallets and handbags are safe. But then that is what they do every time they see someone who does not look quite like them.

At his quayside haunts, he sees some familiar faces. They do not seem to recognise him. He is piqued to discover that although he has been away for only two days, they have already forgotten him. But then a watchman recognises him, and slyly smiles.

'Hey, Toloki, you are back! What happened to you, maan?'

'I live in the settlements now.'

'Ja maan, some vagrant told us that one night you dreamt of a woman, and took your trolley and left. Is she one of the women you met at your funerals?'

'It is a woman from my village. And it is a lie that I dreamt of her and left. I left because I needed a change from the pollution that your vagrant friend was causing – breaking wind and filling the whole place with the smell of rotten cabbage.'

'I agree with you, maan. Me too, I would rather inhale rotten cabbage from a woman's bowels anytime, than from a drunken hobo's.'

Toloki walks away in disgust. He was only trying to be friendly in responding to the watchman's conversation. But that does not give him licence to make crude remarks about Noria, whom he does not even know. He drifts towards the waiting room, and sits on his bench. He fondly watches his ships sail away. He has sat there for many a day, and sailed in those ships. They took him to faraway lands, where he communed with holy men from strange orders that he had never heard of, and took part in their strange rituals, and partook of their strange fare. When he got tired of sailing away in the ships that left the harbour, he came back in those that sailed into the harbour, and was welcomed by throngs of votaries. He sailed mostly during those senseless holidays when people did not bury their dead. When he got tired of sailing, he would just sit and while away time by using his thumbnails to kill the lice that played hide-and-seek in the hems and seams of his costume or home clothes, depending on what he was wearing at the time.

He contemplates his life. Now, his is a world that is far removed from those lonely voyages, and from the merciless slaughter of nits.

Toloki finds himself back in the central business district. He is passing by a stationer's shop when he notices that some art materials are on sale. He enters, and whimsically buys a box of wax crayons and some drawing paper. He has no idea what he wants to do with them. He buys them only because they are there.

He goes to his pastry shop and buys pies and his famous Swiss roll. Outside the store, he buys green onions and dried tarragon leaves. He is going to celebrate New Year's Eve with a royal banquet. Noria can eat the pies and pastries if she does not like his special austere combination. Or she can eat the Swiss roll plain, without relishing them with green onions. After this shopping spree, he thinks of getting some flowers for Noria. He walks towards the part of the city which has roses growing in well-tended sidewalk gardens. But there are too many people walking about. He will not have the opportunity to pick any flowers today. Not even zinnias. All the streets are crowded with New Year's Eve revellers, and the police are on the alert all the time.

He dallies for a while, just watching people. Then in the afternoon, he decides to go back home. He smiles as he realises that he actually thinks of Noria's place as home. It is as though he has lived there all his life.

Back at the settlement, he finds all the children from Madimbhaza's dumping ground playing outside Noria's shack. They have been joined by other settlement children, and there is a lot of screaming, and shouting, and running around the shack, and throwing mud at one another. He greets the children, and Noria walks out of the shack when she hears his voice.

'Oh, Toloki, where did you go?'

'I went to the city, Noria.'

'You should have said so, Toloki, before you left. I was so worried about you. Times are dangerous out there. You never know what might happen to you.'

'I didn't want to wake you up, Noria. You do sleep like a log, you know that.'

The children, Noria tells Toloki, have come to play at her house to give Madimbhaza a break. Children get excited on New Year's Eve, and do not want to sleep until they have seen in the new year at midnight. This means that they will be bothering the old lady until the early hours of the morning. Normally Noria would have gone to look after them at the dumping ground. But as she was worried about the whereabouts of Toloki, she preferred to be at her own shack so that she could wait for him or for news of him.

Toloki laughs.

'What did you think had happened to me?'

'At first I thought you had left me. But when I saw that your trolley with all your property was still here, I had hope that you would come back.'

'I will never leave you, Noria. I am even more convinced of that now that I have been to the city and have visited the places of my old life.'

They sit outside and watch children play. Noria points to a skinny little girl and says that that is Danisa. When she saw all the other children playing at Noria's, she came to play as well. At first, Noria was reminded painfully of her son, for the two children had played together most of the time. But she has forced herself to accept that Danisa will be there, and will be everywhere she wants to be, without her son.

Toloki remembers the crayons and paper that he brought from the city. He takes them out and starts drawing pictures. He draws flowers, and is surprised to see that his hand has not lost its touch. He draws roses that look like those he brought

Noria, the roses that are still very much alive in the bottle that is filled with water inside the shack. He also draws the zinnias that he brought her the other day.

'I was not able to bring you any flowers today, Noria. But you can have these that I have drawn with crayons.'

'I love these even better, Toloki, for they are your own creation.'

As the afternoon progresses, Toloki draws pictures of horses, as he used to do back in the village. Noria says that they are the best pictures that she has seen in all her life. She asks him to draw pictures of children as well. Toloki tries, but he is unable to.

'You remember, Noria, even back in the village I could never draw pictures of human figures.'

Noria jokingly says that maybe she should sing for him, as she used to do for Jwara. After all, Jwara was only able to create through Noria's song. Noria sings her meaningless song of old. All of a sudden, Toloki finds himself drawing pictures of the children playing. Children stop their games and gather around him. They watch him draw colourful pictures of children's faces, and of children playing merry go-round in the clouds. The children from the dumping ground and from the settlement are able to identify some of the faces. These are faces they know, faces of their friends, their own faces. They laugh and make fun of the strange expressions that Toloki has sketched on their purple and yellow and red and blue faces.

The drawing becomes frenzied, as Noria's voice rises. Passers-by stop to watch, and are overcome by warm feelings. It is as though Toloki is possessed by this new ability to create human figures. He breathes heavily with excitement, and his palms are clammy. His whole body tingles, as he furiously gives shape to the lines on the paper. His breathing reaches a crescendo that is broken by an orgasmic scream. This leaves him utterly exhausted. At the same moment, Noria's song stops. The spell breaks, and the passers-by go on their way. Others come and look at Toloki's work, and say it is the work of a genius. In the same way that they read meaning in the shack he and Noria built, they say that the work has profound meaning. As usual, they cannot say what the meaning is. It is not even necessary to say, or even to know, what the meaning is. It is enough only to know that there is a meaning, and it is a profound one.

They had not noticed that Shadrack was one of the spectators. He is pushed in a wheelchair by one of his employees. For the first time, he looks directly at Toloki, and smiles. Toloki detects some condescension, but he does not mind.

'I saw you work. It was a moving experience.'

'Thank you.'

'I didn't think you'd leave the hospital so soon, Bhut'Shaddy. I was planning to go and see you again on New Year's Day.'

'I left against the advice of my doctors. I'll go back after New Year. I had to come back and attend to my business. You know that New Year is a very busy time for business.'

He says that he was on his way to buy more stock for his spaza shop when he saw the crowd gathering. He asked his driver to stop the van, and to wheel him to the shack so that he could see with his own eyes what was happening. He had heard from Noria's homeboys and homegirls of the power she used to have back in the village, and he had never believed the stories. But what he has seen with his own eyes this afternoon has left him dumbfounded. He has never had so much good feeling swelling in his chest before.

'I cannot spoil things between you two. Yours is a creative partnership.'

Shadrack is wheeled back to his van, parked in the street a few yards away. As the van drives away, Noria smiles at Toloki.

'He is right, you know, Toloki.'

Toloki does not respond. He does not understand. But of

course if Noria says that Shadrack is right, he must be right. Then she whispers in his ear.

'And Toloki, don't be ashamed to have dreams about me. It is not dirty to have dreams. It is beautiful. It shows that you are human. We are both human.'

Toloki is embarrassed. How did she know about the dreams? How is she able to read his mind like this? He tries to apologise, and to explain that at least last night he did not have any dreams. But Noria puts her finger on his lips, and tells him that there is no need to say anything.

While these embarrassing exchanges are going on, the children are busy with Toloki's crayons. They are trying to copy the images he has created, and are competing as to whose are better. To escape any further discussion on the merits of dreams, Toloki turns to the children and shows them various techniques of drawing better images.

Late in the afternoon, almost towards dusk, a very long car followed by a truck stops outside Noria's shack. There are many boxes on the truck. A man wearing a black uniform like that of a security guard, or of men whose work is to stand by the entrances of big hotels in the city and open doors for people, alights from the front seat of the limousine and opens the back door. A fat man in a white suit steps out, and pompously waddles towards the shack. Soon all the children are standing around the long white car, admiring it. Other people from the neighbourhood come as well. They have never before seen a car that is as long as a bus.

The fat man is none other than Nefolovhodwe. He greets Toloki and Noria, and laughs in his booming voice.

'They have never seen a car like this before. It is a limousine that I recently imported from America. It is called a Cadillac. Hey, Toloki, my boy, don't you think it's nice that I have come to light up your little miserable lives with my white Cadillac?'

'What do you want from us? Who showed you where we live?'

'Don't be hostile, my boy. When you hear why I came, you will thank me.'

He tells them that he returned from their village that very week. Then he chides them for neglecting their parents.

'You, Toloki, have neglected your mother, and you, Noria, have neglected your father.'

'So now all of a sudden you know who we are, and who our parents are? And you have taken it upon yourself to teach us about our duty to our parents? What about your duty to your real wife and your nine children? Do you think we do not know about you?'

'It is none of your business, ugly boy.'

But Noria is more conciliatory. She wants to know how her father is. Nefolovhodwe relishes being the bearer of news. He tells them that their parents are well, but of course they are much older than he seemed to remember them. Xesibe talks every day of his lost daughter. He still has many cattle, and continues, as before, to be a successful farmer.

'And my mother? How is she?'

'So now you want to know?'

'You can tell me if you like. And then disappear from our lives. You do not impress us at all.'

Noria reprimands Toloki gently, saying that whatever Nefolovhodwe has done to Toloki in the past, he is their visitor at this moment. They must treat him with courtesy.

Toloki, however, is glad to get back at the despicable man, and is rather amazed that a rich and proud man like Nefolovhodwe should just stand there and take all the rudeness being heaped on him. This is not quite the same Nefolovhodwe he remembers, sitting at his huge desk, playing with fleas, and dispensing doses of bad attitude to everyone.

'Well, ugly boy, you will be glad to hear that your mother

too is well. Actually, I went to the village especially to see her.'

'Why would you want to see my mother when you don't know the village people anymore now that you are rich?'

Nefolovhodwe ignores this and goes on to say that he went to Toloki's home. But all the houses were in ruins, as no one had lived there for years. Grass and shrubs had grown all over, and it was impossible to tell that a proud homestead had stood there once upon a time. It was essential that he found Toloki's mother, since he had come all the way from the city to see her. But he had no idea where to look. At the same time, he did not want to go around asking people. He had no desire to renew acquaintances with people he had not seen for many years. Nor did he want to be bothered with stories of how his wife and nine children, who would obviously be adults in their own right by now, were doing. He just wanted to meet Toloki's mother, finish his business with her, and drive to town to the hotel where he was staying.

He had no choice but to go to Xesibe's homestead. Here his quest ended, for he found Toloki's mother living with Xesibe.

'Your parents are cohabiting! In their old age, they have caused a scandal by moving in together.'

Noria and Toloki look at each other, and burst out laughing. They cannot imagine how it came about that Xesibe inherited Jwara's wife, or Toloki's mother inherited That Mountain Woman's husband, depending on how you want to look at it. Nefolovhodwe is unable to understand what is so funny about the whole thing. He waits for them to finish laughing, and tells them that both parents seem to live very well in their rustic simplicity and ignorance of the world, and do not seem to want for anything. Of course, he adds, their tastes are simple rustic tastes. They therefore have no idea of how to spend the wealth that Xesibe has accumulated through his cattle. They are, as a result, misguidedly happy. Their only complaint is that their children have neglected them, and do not even go to the village to see them.

Toloki says that he does not believe that Nefolovhodwe has come all the way from his castle in the suburbs simply to tell them that their parents are missing them. Anyway, how did he know where to find them?

'It was easy. I had people follow you home from a funeral.'

Since he knew from their last confrontation that Toloki was a Professional Mourner, he sent spies to funerals all over the settlements and townships. They went to many funerals, but there was no Professional Mourner there. Toloki is apologetic when he hears this. He says that unfortunately at the moment he is still the only Professional Mourner, and being only one person, he cannot divide himself to attend all the funerals. Nefolovhodwe says he is not concerned with whether funerals have Professional Mourners or not. He is merely telling them of the trouble he went through to find Toloki.

The breakthrough finally came at the last funeral that Toloki and Noria attended. This was the funeral of the patriarch who was killed by his own sons for failing to observe the hair-shaving custom in its proper order. His spies saw the strange figure of a stocky man sitting on a mound, and producing atrocious goatly sounds. From the descriptions that Nefolovhodwe had given them, they knew immediately that this was the man they were looking for. They waited until the funeral was over, and followed Toloki and Noria, first to the funeral meal, and then to their shack. Nefolovhodwe gives a sly smile.

'My spies told me they saw you holding hands with a woman. At the time, I did not know it was this Xesibe's daughter who used to make people happy in the village. Are you two married, or are you copying your parents?'

'Are you married to the young girls you live with? Anyway, what do you want from us?'

'I am in such a good mood that I will ignore your impudence

in calling my wife a young girl. And of course I am married to my wife. I married her in church before a minister. Unlike the old hag in the village for whom I only paid cattle and was deemed to have married by custom. I am a civilized man, my poor ragged children. I do things in a civilized manner. I am refined, and I am cultured.'

'What do you want from us, sir?'

'I brought you your father's things, Toloki.'

'What things?'

'The figurines that he used to make in his workshop.'

'I don't want them. I refuse to accept them.'

Nefolovhodwe signals to the labourers sitting in the back of the truck, and they start unloading the boxes.

'Hey, you can't just dump those things here. What am I going to do with them?'

'You have got to take them, Toloki. Your father wants you to have them.'

'And how do you figure that out? You don't even remember my father.'

Nefolovhodwe, however, reveals that for the past two weeks or so, Jwara has been visiting him in his dreams. At first he was happy, for he thought that this meant he was acquiring the skills and art of necromancy. From his communication with the dead, he expected to learn what the future held for him, and how much more wealth he was going to accumulate. He thought that Jwara would be well-placed to give him advice on such matters, since it was he who advised him to come to the city and make his fortune through the manufacture of coffins in the first place.

But Jwara had other ideas. He had not come to advance Nefolovhodwe's necromantic ambitions. He said that his figurines were suffering. Nefolovhodwe was the only person who could help, by taking them to their rightful owner, namely, Toloki. After all, he had bequeathed them to his only son, and he could not rest in peace in his grave, or join the world of the ancestors, unless the figurines were given to Toloki.

At first, Nefolovhodwe ignored Jwara's demands. He was a busy man, who had to look after his business interests which had expanded far beyond the mere manufacture of coffins. He had now branched out into the creation and marketing of marble and onyx tombstones, of plastic and silk wreaths, and of funeral haute couture for women, especially the widows of millionaires. How could he be expected to spare the time, to go looking for some stupid figurines in some faraway village he never wanted to have anything to do with ever again?

Jwara continued to haunt him. Nefolovhodwe thought that he would resist and win. How could he be defeated by a poor man like Jwara? With all the other people he dealt with in his day-to-day life, his word was final. He was idolised and almost worshipped by people who were in awe of his millions. He was even invited to dinners by white people who held the reins of government. How could he then be expected to obey a mere village blacksmith?

Then his fleas began to die. In his nightly visits, Jwara laughed and danced, and warned that more fleas would die if Nefolovhodwe did not do what he, Jwara, was ordering him to do. He stressed that this was no longer a request, but an order. They were going to duel to the end, until one of them gave up or gave in.

Toloki, hearing this, thinks it serves Nefolovhodwe right if his fleas have died. Whoever heard of a grown man rearing fleas, and playing with them? He had had lice back at the docklands, but they were not there because he was cultivating them. They had just been one of his misfortunes in life. He will admit, however, that he had found it quite entertaining to crush them with his thumbnails. Perhaps there is something in our deriving joy and entertainment from creatures that feed on our blood after all. Maybe he should not judge Nefolovhodwe too harshly on this score, since he had also found joy in his lice. But still the differences cannot be ignored. His joy was in the dying of his lice, whereas Nefolovhodwe's is in the living of his fleas.

Nefolovhodwe had to give in when he lost some of the champion performers in his flea circus. He drove one of his more durable luxury cars to the village, and saw the ruins that were Toloki's home. When he finally found Toloki's mother, she said that she did not know what had happened to the figurines, and did not care. Those figurines had destroyed her family life, she said, so she had never been interested in knowing their fate. The last she remembered, they were in the workshop. The workshop was now just a pile of stones. Since all the blacksmith equipment was sold to other blacksmiths, no one ever bothered to go there.

Nefolovhodwe rounded up a few labourers, and proceeded to excavate the site of the workshop. To his surprise, among the rocks and debris, they dug up many figurines. Some were buried in the soil. And all of them were glittering as if they had been freshly polished. Yet no one had disturbed them for all those years.

Toloki is not in the least surprised to hear that the figurines had remained untouched for so many years, without people trying to help themselves to them. He remembers that many years ago, when Jwara was still strong, and Noria was a regular singer at their creative sessions, thieves once broke into the workshop. They stole everything they could carry, including his sets of bellows, but did not touch any of the figurines. At first, Jwara was happy that the figurines had not been stolen.

'The spirits that made me create these wonderful works are too strong for thieves. No one can touch these figurines.'

But Toloki's mother dampened his spirits by suggesting that the thieves had ignored the figurines because they were wise enough to see that they were useless.

'What would any self-respecting thief do with the worthless iron monsters that you spend your precious time making, instead of making things that will support your family?'

Those critical comments started some sobering self-doubt in Jwara. What if the woman was right? Were the thieves making a critical statement about the value of his art when they stole everything else, but neglected his works which were conspicuously displayed on the shelves for everyone to see? He became very angry with the thieves for not stealing his figurines.

When Jwara invaded Nefolovhodwe's dreams and ordered him to fetch the figurines from the village and deliver them to Toloki, he forgot to mention just how many there were. Nefolovhodwe had thought that they would fit into just one or two boxes. But after they had dug out everything, he found that they were so many that they would not fit in his car. He wondered how Jwara had managed to create all these works, and where he had got the iron and sometimes brass to make so many figurines. Or did they perhaps multiply on their own, giving birth to more metal monsters?

He decided to leave a few men to guard the site, and drove back to his hotel in town. There he phoned his office in the city, and asked them to send a truck, along with many strong labourers, and many boxes. The next day the truck arrived. The figurines were loaded, and Nefolovhodwe and his men drove back to the city.

'Now that I have given you your figurines, please tell your father to stop bothering me.'

'I have said that I am not accepting them. What does my father want me to do with these ugly things?'

Noria calls Toloki aside, and whispers in his ear.

'Toloki, the figurines are not ugly. Remember that my spirit is in them too. And we must never use that painful word – ugly.'

When Toloki turns to Nefolovhodwe again, his anger has dissipated. He tells him that he will accept the figurines.

'I am glad that this Xesibe's daughter who used to give pleasure to all and sundry has talked sense into your head. Our elders say that we should build a kraal around the word of the deceased, because it is precious like cattle used to be. When your father says you must have the figurines, then you must have the figurines.'

Toloki says that although he will accept them, he does not know what he will do with them, or where he will put them. There are too many to fit into even a four-roomed township matchbox house, let alone their small shack.

'I thought of that, ugly boy. I took the liberty of showing some of these figurines to two friends of mine. One is an art dealer, and the other the chair of a board of trustees that runs an art gallery and a museum.'

On examining the work, the art dealer said that the figurines looked quite kitschy, but added that kitsch was the 'in' thing for collectors with taste this season. It was likely that this trend would continue for the next two years or so. The museum man disagreed. He said the work was folksy rather than kitsch. And folksy works were always in demand with trendy collectors. Although the two men disagreed on how to define Jwara's works, they both agreed that it had some value. The problem, of course, was that because there were so many works, they would not fetch a high price. But there might be individual pieces with special features that would make them stand apart. These would certainly fetch a higher price.

Neither Toloki nor Noria understand what Nefolovhodwe is talking about. Toloki wonders how a simple village carpenter with little or no education has managed to acquire this vast amount of knowledge. The information that the despicable man is dishing out to them, with utmost pomposity, is absolutely meaningless to them. All Toloki wants is for Nefolovhodwe to just disappear, and leave them playing with their little guests in peace.

'Don't bother your simple heads if you don't understand the subtle disagreement between the two experts. I had to learn some of these things when I became a multi-millionaire. If you are interested in getting rid of these things in a manner that will profit you, I can call my friends first thing in the morning, and ask them to come for them. And, Toloki, don't forget to tell your father that I did all these things to help you, at great expense too. He must now stop haunting me.'

'You know that I don't accept charity. I am going to pay you back every cent that you spent to bring these things to me.'

'No! No! Please don't pay me back. I don't want to be haunted by Jwara again. Right now, it's going to take me a long time to bring my fleas to international performing standards again, after losing some of my best champions.'

The workers have finished packing the boxes next to the shack. They are so many that they occupy space that is many times bigger than the shack in height, breadth and length. Toloki opens one of the boxes, and the children are immediately fascinated by the figurines. Even those who were admiring Nefolovhodwe's limousine lose interest in it, and crowd around the boxes instead. Toloki and Noria take a few of the figurines out of the boxes and give them to the children. Some of the figurines are so strange and sinister-looking that they are afraid that they might scare the children. But to their surprise the children love them. They look at them and laugh.

Everyone is so engrossed in the figurines that no one notices Nefolovhodwe and his truck drive away. He honks the hooter of his limousine, which produces a few bars of a hymn that is an all-time favourite at funerals. But no one pays any attention. Everyone is absorbed in the figurines. The children are falling into such paroxysms of laughter that they roll around on the ground. Toloki is amazed to see that the figurines give pleasure to the children in the same way that Noria gave pleasure to the whole community back in the village.

Just before midnight, Toloki takes out his cakes and onions. When he bought them, he had not known that they were going to have so many visitors. He had thought that they would have a banquet in the oak dining room after taking a long walk in their garden – just the two of them. Now he has to share the cakes with the children. He gives each one a small piece, which simply melts in the mouths of the children like sacramental wafers. Noria tries the Swiss roll with green onion, and falls in love with the combination. Then she chews the tarragon leaves with Toloki, and enjoys them as well. The children are more concerned with the figurines, and their laughter remains unabated.

Toloki and Noria have still not worked out what to do with the figurines. They decide that they will keep one of the figurines in their shack, next to Toloki's roses, to remind themselves where they came from.

'With the rest, Noria, perhaps we should sell them as Nefolovhodwe suggested, and take the money to Madimbhaza's dumping ground.'

'Or we could let them stay here with us, and bring happiness and laughter to the children. We could build a big shack around them, and the children could come and laugh whenever they felt like it.'

At twelve midnight exactly, bells from all the churches in the city begin to ring. Hooters are blaring in all the streets. The settlement people burst into a cacophony: beating pots and pans and other utensils together, while shouting 'Happe-e-e-e New Year!' The din is reminiscent of an off-tune steel band. At every street corner, tyres are burning.

* * *

Two hours after midnight, we are still shouting 'Happe-e-ee!' We revel staggeringly past Noria's shack. All is still. There is no movement. No light can be seen through the cracks of the door. The children have gone back to their homes. We look at the mountain of boxes that dwarfs the shack. We do not touch. We just look and marvel. Our children have told us about the monsters that make people happy. Maybe it is the drink, but it seems that we can see them through the boxes, shimmering like fool's gold. Not even the most habitual thieves among us lift a finger towards the boxes.

Somehow the shack seems to glow in the light of the moon, as if the plastic colours are fluorescent. Crickets and other insects of the night are attracted by the glow. They contribute their chirps to the general din of the settlement. Tyres are still burning. Tyres can burn for a very long time. The smell of burning rubber fills the air. But this time it is not mingled with the sickly stench of roasting human flesh. Just pure wholesome rubber.